Wend

Wendy Steele lives on a hillside in Wales. She can see the mountains from a place on her land where one day, she'll build a straw bale writing room.

She worked in the City, BC (Before Children) but since 1999 has indulged her creative side, training in natural therapies, belly dance and writing, culminating in her first novel, 'Destiny of Angels - First book in the Lilith Trilogy' and in 2012, her first non-fiction title ' Wendy Woo's Year - A Pocketful of Smiles'.

Wendy is passionate about writing magical realism, bringing real people and real magic to her readers. The Standing Stone Series are the latest books in this genre, linking three women across time and space with the goddesses who can inspire them.

Wendy lives with her partner, Mike, and four cats. When not writing or teaching dance, she spends her days renovating her house, clearing her land and, when time and weather allows, sitting on her riverbank, breathing in the beauty of nature.

Also by Wendy Steele

Fiction

Destiny of Angels
First Book In The Lilith Trilogy

Wrath of Angels
Second Book In The Lilith Trilogy

Too Hot for Angels
Six (eXtra Sexy) Extended Scenes
(The Lilith Trilogy)

Turn Down The Heat
A Short Story Anthology

Into The Flames
A Short Story Anthology

The Standing Stone - Home For Christmas
First Novella In The Standing Stone Series

Non-Fiction

Wendy Woo's Year - A Pocketful of Smiles
101 ideas for a happy year and a happy you

The Standing Stone

Silence Is Broken

Wendy Steele

www.wendysteele.com

Text Copyright © Wendy Steele 2015
Published 2015, in Great Britain,
by Phoenix & The Dragon

All rights reserved. No part of this publication may be reproduced, stored in a retrieval system, or transmitted in any form or by any means, electronic, mechanical, photocopy, recording or otherwise, without prior written permission of the copyright owner. Nor can it be circulated in any form of binding or cover other than that in which it is published and without similar condition including this condition being imposed on a subsequent purchaser.

Please visit www.wendysteele.com
for contact details

ISBN 978-1512399226

British Cataloguing Publication data:
A catalogue record of this book is available from the British Library

This book is also available as an ebook
Please visit
www.wendysteele.com
for more details.

Kathleen Beatrice Steele
(1920 – 2014)

I will always remember the good times

Home

Think of me in this barren landscape
Think of me, on this hill
Far away from love and friendship
Think of me, if you will.

Spare a tear for my weighty burden
Digging new this foreign land
Felling trees to build my homestead.
Hearth and home made with this hand.

But the earth, it is the same earth
And the sea 'tween shore and shore
Gives me hope in times of hardship
That I'm coming home once more.

Coming home, I'm coming home
Coming home from distant shore.

Think of me as I bring in the harvest
Plucking crop from land and tree
Tending flock and growing family
Dry your eyes and think of me.

Trees and hilltops, plants and flowers
Glossy stars that light Her dome
Where I live in Nature's beauty
That to me, is truly home.

But the earth, it is the same earth
And the sea 'tween shore and shore
Gives me hope in times of hardship
That I'm coming home once more.

Coming home, I'm coming home
Coming home from distant shore.

The Standing Stone – Silence Is Broken

Chapter 1

Opening her eyes, Rachel shivered. She lay flat on the grass and far above her hung Inanna's girdle, magnificent in its dazzling abundance. Her duffel coat lay beside her and she stood up, fumbling her way into the sleeves and raiding her pockets for gloves. She stamped her feet to keep warm as she covered her frozen digits and saw a light, swaying in the darkness, making its way up the mound.

"Here you are," said Marcus, breathless and sweating. His eyes were red and swollen and his cheeks stained with salt.

"Yes, I love it up here," said Rachel, opening her arms to the heavens and twirling around until she fell to the ground, dizzy and giggling.

"Let me have a go," said Marcus. Head back, he grinned as he turned again and again until he joined Rachel in a heap on the grass.

"What happened to the man who couldn't resist a grass slope to roll down or the challenge of a river swing? Or the man who changed his hair style and facial hair like he changed his shirt?" said Rachel.

"What happened to the woman who came to wash my back in the bathroom but could never resist getting in? Or the woman who played Debussy on the piano while I made fresh pasta and always wore stockings rather than tights?" said Marcus.

They sat with their backs to the Standing Stone, looking up at the splendour above them. Rachel put her hand on Marcus' arm and he covered it with his own. "Who knows?" said Rachel, "But shall we try to find them together?"

Marcus stood up, pulling her with him. He clicked on his torch and, still holding Rachel's hand, began walking down the mound. "I'm taking you home," he said, "Home for Christmas."

They descended together, their arms bumping and their breath entwining as if neither wished to stray too far in case this peaceful, contented spell was broken.

Marcus brought in all the cut wood he could find and soon had the burner blazing. With tea and toast they sat close together, remembering the comfortable stillness they had shared on the mound, both hoping to replicate it but afraid to speak.

The next morning, Marcus gathered holly and mistletoe and cut streamers of ivy and together they cleaned and decorated their home with the symbols of mid winter. Rachel ransacked drawers and cupboards for all the glass and pottery receptacles she could find and filled them with tea lights.

That evening they lounged on old duvets and cushions on the floor. In the glow of candle light, they listened to music and sipped a smooth Merlot.

Rachel accepted Marcus' arms around her and she rested her head on his shoulder. "I'd forgotten how comforting it is to be held by you."

Marcus pulled her closer. "I'm sorry."

"We're both to blame. I get my practical head on and can't get past it sometimes!"

The Standing Stone – Silence Is Broken

"I've neglected you, I know," said Marcus, "but losing Mum and Dad and Will...It's as if a piece of me went with them. It's left me weak and vulnerable."

"It's okay," said Rachel, "I wanted to help and I thought if you kept going, looked forward to a new start...but you've not grieved yet."

Marcus sat up, drawing Rachel onto his lap while he leaned against the sofa. "Neither have you," he said, gently, "I don't blame you, you know that don't you?"

She let her head rest on his chest as two years of tears fell down her cheeks, bringing with them the emotional anguish of the loss of their baby. His short life played out in her mind; the joy and excitement of finding out she was pregnant, the news of the death of Marcus' mum and dad and his brother, Will and then finally, the tiny, silent, inert bundle taken from her arms.

"I'm so sorry," she whispered.

"Please don't," said Marcus, rocking her gently, "I was so wrapped up in my own grief, I couldn't take any more."

They cried together for the loss of their son, as the candles flickered in their holders and the cold winter's night began to freeze.

Rachel woke the next morning and snuggled closer to Marcus. Last night, once their tears had abated, Marcus had kissed her with a passion she had forgotten and they spent the evening rediscovering every part of each other until they fell into an exhausted, blissful sleep.

Wrapping her side of the duvet around her, Rachel knelt up to the tiny window high in the gable. A landscape of glittering frost greeted her.

When Candy opened her eyes, she sat on the dirt with the lever on the wall in front of her. As her brain took in her suited, booted and gloved body and touched the PD, visor down, on her head, the needle on the silver disc touched the second red segment and Candy stood, slamming the lever to the ground.

She waited at the guard post beside the metal box.

As Aaron stood before her, she slid the security band over his wrist and flipped back her visor. "Hello, Aaron," she said, "I think you and I should talk, don't you?"

Aaron's startled expression and miming of shutting her visor made Candy laugh, until a movement behind her and a cloth over her mouth, turned her world black.

A throbbing pain in her forehead and a painfully dry mouth roused Candy from her enforced slumber. Cold metal gripped her ankles and pinned her head to the table on which she lay. Her torso was trapped beneath something heavy which also pinned her arms to her sides. Panic rose in her throat and she suppressed the scream that built inside her as she feared her worst nightmare was a reality. She blinked frantically, checking to ensure her eyes were open as she tried to focus on her surroundings but all was dark. Nausea squirmed in her stomach until she forced herself to take the best deep breath she could and, as she breathed out, she began to count her beats.

She was alive, her beats confirmed it, and though blind and scared, she remembered the feeling of cool fresh air on her face and the cold crystal texture of the Standing Stone and she took Comfort from it while she continued to count.

Without warning, the table slowly tilted, her head rising until she sat, her legs straight out in front of her. She cried out at the brightness of the Screen, screwing up her eyes at first before tears burst from them at the joyous realisation that she could see.

She recognised two of the three faces which peered at her from the Screen and her heart leapt with realisation and annoyance. Aaron stood on one side of Abraham Adams Manager 37 and as she looked at his pale blue eyes she berated herself for her stupidity. Shocked by the message Aaron had left her, in the dirt at Station 23, Candy had ignored his 'A' name so only now, as he stood beside AAM37, did the preposterous idea of a first born on guard duty manifest itself to her.

AAM37 spoke from the screen. "You are Candy Guard 14387. You were given the opportunity to improve guard security at station 23 but this was not forthcoming."

"I tried!" cried Candy, "I did my best!"

"You were also seen Below without your visor in place."

All three faces stared at her. The third face was clear skinned, pale and almost oval with a smooth bald pate above it. The eyes were small and slanted, viewing Candy as if she were a specimen in a jar.

What could she say? She couldn't deny it and yet, she wanted to preserve the secret she had found down the long dark passageway. The Standing Stone, protruding from the dark grey wall, was her only hope for the future.

"It was an accident," she said, "I hadn't snapped it quite shut when I left the Comfort Cubicle. I felt air on my face. It's very hot standing in a bio suit for twelve hours Below."

"You disobeyed the Lesson."

"Yes, but not on purpose and not until I knew it was safe."

The small bald man shook his head and looked at AAM37 while Aaron stared at her, horror visible on his face.

"So you take full responsibility for the breach of security at station 23?" asked AAM37.

"Yes," said Candy, without hesitation.

Abraham Adams Manager 37 sat back, crossed his arms and stared at her. His reserved expression had gone and he was almost smiling. "So you will stay silent about your guard partner to protect One and yet disobey a Lesson which is set in place for the good of All, even knowing the punishment this brings?"

"Paul's simple, he doesn't understand," said Candy.

"Paul is your friend?"

The Standing Stone – Silence Is Broken

"Of course not. I have no friends." Now she had said it, admitted the truth, explained her disobedience, she felt relieved. Fear of being caught no longer weighed her down. "He's another human being," she added, "but one I see every day. I suppose I care what happens to him."

"Yet you allow the All to suffer," said AAM37, "Don't you care about the All?"

"How can I? I can't hold them or listen to their sadness or see the pain of frustration in their eyes!"

AAM37 nodded. The table tilted back as the Screen went out and Candy was plunged into darkness.

Fern awoke with her head pressed against the Standing Stone. She turned and all she saw was the crouched figures of both villages, prostrate at her feet.

Adalwin rose and came to join her, Geirr scurrying in his wake. Adalwin took her hand and gestured to the tribes with the other. "They all believe you are a Goddess," said Geirr, translating for Adalwin, "I already knew."

He bowed to her.

"What happened?" she asked Adalwin, turning to Geirr.

"They saw you change, if you please, my lady," said Geirr.

Adalwin interrupted him. "Your face was like a thousand faces, changing every moment and your voice shook the earth."

Fern looked at the villagers before her, some peering up to see what she would do. "Did I sing?"

"You did, my lady," answered Geirr.

"And the song?"

"One of our own, it were. Just the final verse," said Geirr.

She beckoned to the villagers to stand and torches were passed and lit amongst a murmur of conversations until a voice rang out, like pure clean energy, into the air and over the mountains.

"Trees and hilltops, plant and flowers
Glossy stars that light Her dome
Where I live, in Nature's beauty
 That to me, is truly home."

As Adalwin sang, Fern knew what she must do. Though mid-winter, with all the hardships and privations that cold season brings, it was also the time to bear the light, ignite the fire, the passion and the resilience of the people, to plan and look forward to warm days in the sun and welcome the light home. The Tall Folk had similar traditions, so Geirr said, and if she was the Goddess they believed her to be, then they would do as she said.

"Please hear me," said Fern. All were silent before her. Some returned to bended knees.

"Stand up, for we are all equals," she said, "We are one tribe!"

Geirr translated and eyes turned to Nia and Adalbern.

"We are all people!" cried Fern, "Let us love and thank the Great Mother together and welcome home the light!"

Women from her tribe cried out in agreement and soon both tribes were cheering into the cold winter's night. The drums began and the Tall Folk drummers joined them, following the torches down the mound. As one tribe, they returned to the village and as one tribe, they fed the ritual fire, its flames rising higher than the tallest round house, shooting sizzling fireworks into the dome of stars. Women from both villages brought out food and welcomed neighbours and strangers alike to partake of the midwinter feast.

Once his father was seated, Adalwin sat by Fern and she leaned on his shoulder as the songs began. She didn't know exactly what the villagers had seen by the Standing Stone but, at least for now, everyone was content and happy to be welcoming home the light. She needed to speak to Nia, but not tonight. Her experience at the Standing Stone had filled her with questions but now was not the time for answers. Tonight she would sit by the ritual fire and celebrate the Great Mother and her bounty in song and dance.

The next morning, Nia sat with Fern on her sleeping mat as they watched the villagers, making their preparations, bustling from house to house.

"It was your mother who suggested to the Council that after the mid winter ritual, we share our homes. Half the number of fires are lit but they keep twice as many people warm," said Nia.

"Tell me more about my mother."

"First, you must hear of your mother's line. I learned all I know from Ciara, before she left to join the ancestors. Your mother's mother's mother's mother lived on this Land with her parents. They were the first to build a home and live with Nature the way we do."

"So mother's family started the village?"

Nia nodded. "Six seasons passed by which time four families had joined them. One night, at the spring ritual, while all around danced and sang in the firelight, your kin was led to the forest by a force she could not see and there she found an elfin baby."

"What does that mean?"

"Let me tell you," said Nia, crawling over to put more wood on the fire. "Your kin brought the baby home and raised her as her own. She named her Willow. As the seasons went by, Willow was a happy, thoughtful child, content with her own company as well as running around with the other children. Raised as daughter, Willow repeated the rituals of her kin but also brought ideas to the village. She showed the men how to build the cart and the women, how to collect seeds for planting."

"But she was just a child," insisted Fern.

"Not just a child. A child's body filled with the knowing and seeing of a wise woman."

"But how?"

"All we know is she was your mother's mother's mother and, since then, the wise women of this tribe have been of your line."

Fern stared at the floor, her eyes unseeing.

"I did my best," continued Nia, "Your mother and I were good friends and I promised her I would look after you and Rowan."

The Standing Stone – Silence Is Broken

"And I shouted at you on the mound," said Fern, looking away, "I should be thanking you, I'm sorry."

"Your words were the right words, Fern, for you are your mother's daughter. I am the one who is sorry and will bend to your wishes." She bowed her head to Fern.

"Stop it," said Fern, trying to laugh, "I'm not a wise woman or a goddess."

"I saw you on the mound and I know you are more than I could ever be. Maybe your kin were not elfin but spirit, a reincarnation of the goddess of the forest herself. Either way, you are special Fern and your tribe needs you."

Chapter 2

Rachel collapsed onto the sofa, sweating and exhausted as Marcus lit the fire. They had spent the whole morning cutting and splitting wood as the icy cold made their eyes run and their ears burn. The inglenook piled high with split logs and the basket full of kindling was testament to their hard work.

As the first logs turned to burning embers and Rachel stacked up the burner, they sat drinking tea.

"We make a good team," said Marcus, squeezing her thigh, "I'm so sorry I put you through all this."

"We're making a fresh start," said Rachel, "and I'm glad we started today."

Marcus nodded.

"So no more secrets. No hiding bits of paper or letting me believe something because it's easier for you," she teased.

Marcus leaned against the sofa. "Then, I have a confession."

His serious face made Rachel's stomach twist and she heard her heart beating in her ears.

"First, you must know, I love you Rachel. I know you believe me when I say I didn't know what I wanted any more. The pit of despair held me deep within it."

"I know," said Rachel, "and you extolling the virtues of a life in the country was a way to keep the despair at bay while not facing or dealing with your grief."

"Yeah, and the drinking, all of it, all avoidance tactics. But I did contemplate leaving you and the painful memories behind me."

"Leaving me?"

Marcus nodded.

"Why?"

"I thought if I abandoned the past, I could live in the future."

"Without me?"

"I'm sorry but it was how I was thinking. When I saw you, I saw our wedding day with my family...and baby Jack."

"Where would you have gone?" said Rachel, her bottom lip trembling as she fought to keep calm.

Marcus squirmed beneath her intense gaze. "So, this is the other part I didn't tell you. You found the paperwork for Dad's building company and the properties in this country."

"The sheets I was meant to find?"

Marcus nodded. "But mum and dad were buying, renovating and selling property before I was born. I own a portfolio of over fifty houses and apartments."

She began counting her beats and the surety of the counting steadied her heartbeat, forcing back the nausea and allowing her to breathe. And think.

The face of the Great Mother Binah filled her mind and, for the first time in her adult life, Candy didn't feel alone. This person, goddess, mother had given her a family, a connection to her birth mother and her own mother before her and this brought Comfort to Candy. She didn't understand all Binah said, how she, Rachel and Fern had touched the Standing Stone and arrived together in another place with Binah but that didn't matter. Binah filled her mind with a past she had not known but which had brought her to this place and time.

During her childhood in the Learning Zone, receiving Lessons from the Teacher on the Screen, Candy was taught a brief history of the planet. The world, she was taught, was created by a Great Maker. He created mountains, lakes and seas and set the sun in the sky to warm the earth by day and the moon to cool it by night. This was the First Age. In the Second Age, he made the first people. They were primitive, roaming the earth, killing animals to eat and living in tents. They had no language and no understanding of the world so the Great Maker froze the land and started again. Six more Ages passed some ending in ice, others plague or violent volcanic disruption until the Ninth Age. These people learned about their world and the resources it held and became prosperous. Candy recalled the photos of smiling families sat at tables laden with food she did not know and of buildings, motorised vehicles, aeroplanes and space rockets.

She was taught, by the Teacher on the Screen, that people acquired knowledge and they confronted the Great Maker, asking for more resources and information. The Great Maker was angry at their presumption and sent devastation upon the Ninth Age but the Company were clever and built the Dome to shelter All from the destruction. This was not the Tenth Age but the Age of the Dome.

Candy shut her eyes and a tear pressed through her lids and slid past her ear. Fed information from the Screen, she had no means to ascertain its truthfulness but, since finding the Standing Stone, she saw the inadequacy of the Lessons. All the unanswered questions she struggled with, were her mind querying the validity of everything she had been taught.

Once old enough for Self Study, she had found information on the Screen herself which contradicted her original teaching. The sun was a huge hot star while the moon, earth and other planets orbited the sun. Maybe all these planets were created by the Great Maker but she doubted it and this increased her uncertainty about the creation of the Dome. Waves of despair racked her mind as she lay silently weeping into the darkness.

With Geirr, spiritual guide to Adalbern, Adalwin's father, acting as translator, Fern talked to Adalwin about the tradition of sharing a hearth in preparation for the long winter ahead.

"We managed last year," said Adalwin, "If it gets too cold and the wood piles run low, my father has agreed for our tribe to be housed in the great house."

"As you wish," said Fern, "Geirr, I want to speak to Adalwin alone."

"But you can't...," began Geirr. With one glance at Fern's face, he left them.

"Come," said Fern, beckoning Adalwin towards the forest.

They walked on, around and over tree stumps, into the denser wooded land before sliding down the river bank and sitting above the gushing water. The earth on the bank was moist and warm enough to mark so, in pictures, gestures and facial expressions, Fern told Adalwin what Nia had told her about her kin. She tried to express her worries and fears about such a responsibility until Adalwin took both her hands and held them to him.

In Fern's language he said, "You woman." He touched his heart. "Adalwin's woman."

As Adalwin smiled at Fern her worries melted away. In his simple, honest words he was right. It didn't matter how the villagers saw her. She was Fern and all her female kin before her and with this comforting knowledge, she made a decision.

That evening Fern spoke to Nia. "Together, Nia. I want to share what you have carried alone for so long."

"You already know much," said Nia, clasping Fern to her, "but I will teach you all I know."

"Thank you," said Fern, holding her tightly.

"And will you teach me?" asked Nia.

Before Fern could answer, Rowan, Fern's younger sister landed on the sleeping mat with them.

"Bramble says you're a goddess!" she squealed, "Belle shushed her but I could see she believed it too! After your face flickering all funny on the mound, that's what they all believe! You're not really a goddess, are you?"

"It's time you learned where you came from," said Fern, Rowan's black hair resting in her lap, "It's time you too learned of your mother and your kin." She stroked the raven braids as she continued, "Our mother's mother's mother's mother lived on this Land with her parents. They were the first..."

Chapter 3

"You could have gone to live in one of those properties," said Rachel.

Marcus nodded. "I'm afraid I contemplated staging a fake suicide."

"What?" cried Rachel.

"I know," said Marcus, "Please listen."

He held her to him. She could feel his heart pounding as he tried to explain.

"I was so unhappy and you were so...busy."

Rachel let the tears fall, a blessed release from the tension his words had brought and, in that moment, the face and words of Binah, the Great Mother came to her. "When your mind is open and you learn, you accumulate wisdom."

She spoke softly to Marcus but with a resolution that filled her body and joined her directly to the earth.

"In the past, I used action and focus, determination and selfless hard work to alleviate the pain. By planning and putting those plans into action, I believed the pain would go and I would be happy. In fact, I tried to make us happy. *I tried to make you happy!*"

She buried her face in his jumper.

"I know," said Marcus, stroking her long dark hair, "I know."

Once the burner was roaring, the radiators warmed and they shared a bubble bath, legs wrapped around each other as they kissed cheeks, lips and necks. Pent up salty tears fell into the fragrant water and years of pain and grief dispersed among the suds.

That evening, Marcus made burritos, their first Mexican meal in Wales and Rachel wallowed in the bliss of having Marcus by her side.

"You being so capable made me feel worse," said Marcus.

"I can see that now."

"I only wanted to leave because I didn't want to hurt you any more. I knew I was but couldn't stop it."

"I know. I have a question. Any chance that one of these properties of yours is in hot sunshine with a private pool?"

"Have you any idea how much trouble you are in?" whispered a voice by Candy's left ear.

Startled, she tried to turn her head but a sharp pain in her forehead stopped her, as metal dug into skin. She lay back, panting and blind as the voice continued.

"You're still here because you fascinate them," said the voice, "Though tutored and nurtured by robots and the emotionless Screen, you show empathy and compassion to someone you don't know. No one who is brought here does anything but scream for their own life. Sssh, don't speak. The Screen is coming on."

As the voice whispered the final words, the top half of the table began to rise and she shut her eyes as the Screen shone brightly. She opened them, trying to look to the side to see who was with her but she could see nothing except the round bald headed man from the previous Screening.

"Candy Guard 14387, you are charged with leaving station 23 unguarded during your shift of duty. How do you plead?"

"What?"

"Candy Guard 14387, you are charged with disobeying the Lesson 'One who goes Below must wear a bio suit, gloves, boots and Personal Dome at all times.' How do you plead?"

"What are you talking about?"

She wriggled in her fastenings, her skin chaffing and bleeding against the metal.

The Screen went black and then immediately the face of Abraham Adams Manager 37 appeared.

"Candy Guard 14387, answer the charge."

"No!" cried Candy.

She heard a gasp at her side.

"No!" she cried again, "I've always worked hard and done my best but I don't understand! Why is wanting to understand so bad? Why is trying to protect One of the All so difficult for *you* to understand? Weren't you taught that the Age of the Dome was built for All?"

She was in the groove now and the questions came tumbling out.

"Why couldn't I learn with other children? On the earth Before there were schools so the children could talk and help each other so why are we set apart? Why must I wear a PD as the Lesson says when I know the air is safe to breathe? Why do..."

The Standing Stone – Silence Is Broken

"Enough!" cried AAM37.

His brow was furrowed and he glared at Candy as she whimpered and tried to turn her head.

"It is the ruling of One, Abraham Adams Manager 37, that Candy Guard 14387 is a reject. Despite her tutoring, provided freely by the goodness of the Company, she has failed to be a responsible One and is, therefore, a danger to All. Candy Guard 14387, you will be blinded and ejected from the Dome."

Nia opened her hearth to two families from the village, both parents coping with a small baby and a toddler. Once Rowan was bedded down, she fell asleep quickly, the excitement of the prospect that she too could be a goddess or, better still in her view, a fairy, tiring her despite the cries of the babies and grumbles of the toddlers around her.

Fern wondered for a while whether filling their home with small children was Nia's idea to dissuade Fern from getting to know Adalwin but she dismissed the notion as she watched Nia rocking a baby while his parents slept for the first night in weeks.

She whispered to Nia, not wanting to disturb the child. "Did you have a love, Nia, a man you couldn't bear to be apart from?"

Nia smiled and nodded. She stood up, pacing and rocking the baby as she spoke. "When your mother and I were children, there were two other families in the tribe. Your father was the eldest son of one and my love, Neirin, the eldest of the other."

"What happened?"

"They were best friends, two strong boys, eldest sons eager to show their prowess. They often wrestled and their fathers and the other men encouraged it."

Nia sat beside Fern, looking into the fire, lost in her memory.

"One day, your father was losing the fight, my Neirin having blossomed into a man that winter, but your father gathered his strength and pushed Neirin off him with his legs. Neirin went backwards, hitting his head on a rock. Nothing would stop the blood and he never awakened to say farewell before he died."

"I'm sorry."

"No need, no need."

"Why did my father leave? When mother died, why didn't he stay?"

"You must understand, the accident affected him greatly. He and Neirin were close friends. Your mother comforted your father and you were conceived and you brought them joy and happiness but when your mother died, your father became morose and distanced himself from the tribe. Rumours began that he had infected your mother with his misery somehow, which is nonsense but knowing he wanted to leave, I offered to take care of you and Rowan."

"So he's alive?"

Nia frowned. "I don't know. He left with his parents and two younger sisters but in all the seasons of Rowan's life, I have not seen him once, not any of them."

The Standing Stone – Silence Is Broken

Fern snuggled under her skins with Rowan and lay thinking about the father she never knew before she drifted off to sleep.

She was awoken by shouts and scuffling and opened her eyes to a misty wet dawn. A figure was being carried to the fire, a man whose face sprouted jet black curly hair and whose body was wrapped in skins.

"I went to check the water for the animals," said a voice, rising above the commotion, "Must have been the cold last night."

"Take him away," ordered Nia, instructing the men farther from the fire, "He must warm up slowly if he's to live. Go back to your work, all of you. I'll call Council if there is news."

Fern bound her chest and arms with fabric and fur and put on her sheepskin trousers before climbing over Rowan to Nia. "Will he live?"

"I don't know. If he stirs, we'll try warm soup. Here, hold his head while I get on."

Fern sat with the stranger's head in her lap, marvelling at the hairiness of his face and cheekily wondering if he was hairy all over. He was older than Adalwin she knew, as he had lines around his eyes but there were no streaks of white in his thick black mane so, he wasn't as old as Adalbern.

As the stranger stirred, Nia gave him sips of soup from a wooden spoon and he gulped down the liquid and opened his eyes. Like balls of charcoal, his jet black irises sat on a palate of red and Fern wondered how long he had been out in the cold.

The man tried to speak but she did not understand his words. At their obvious bemusement, the man tried to sit up but fell back, exhausted.

Geirr was summoned and smug in his capacity as translator, he listened to the man's words. His face quickly lost its smile. Geirr's hair was nearly gone, though he was not an old man so he wore a fur hat for all seasons. It pushed down his big ears, rather than covering them, making him look like an overheated goat. He rubbed them as he conveyed the hairy man's message.

"His village was attacked. He escaped and walked for ten moons. There were many fighting men. He does not know how many died but he saw his woman and child murdered and ran into the forest. He has been walking up river."

"Thank you, Geirr," said Nia, "I will call Council."

"Should we not ask Adalbern to join us?" said Fern. "This affects him and his people too."

"Of course, Adalbern must be invited."

Chapter 4

Driving to work on Christmas Eve, Rachel smiled as she recalled Marcus' laughing the previous evening. He'd chuckled and roared, trying to compose himself before launching into a fresh bout of giggles. Tears streamed from his eyes as he held his sides and laughed. Why wouldn't she think about a place in the sun after the efforts it took them to keep warm? It was a perfectly sensible question.

Talking long into the night, the realisation had crept over Rachel that they were well off, very well off indeed. At first she was scared at the prospect of such wealth, worried by her parents belief that you could buy anything you wanted with money, including love and happiness but the more they talked, she could see, they could do anything they wanted and help a lot of people.

This morning Marcus wanted her to call in sick but she wouldn't let Ffion down so he relented and promised her a surprise when she came home. She mentioned the Christmas drink in the pub and he encouraged her to go. He wanted her to make friends, he said.

The morning in the hair salon was swept along by a medley of carols, paper hats and tinkling reindeer antlers. Rachel's later clients were happy to come earlier and have Siân and Beth's attention. The excitement grew when Ffion arrived. There were gifts for all the staff and chocolate biscuits for the clients.

Ffion locked up, relieving Rachel of the keys. As they followed the other staff down the hight street, Ffion pressed an envelope into Rachel's hands.

"A little bonus," she said, holding Rachel's arm.

"Really, there's no need," said Rachel.

"Please, please, you've been wonderful, truly an angel sent to help me," insisted Ffion, "I feel so much better for taking my time in the morning especially if Mr Bump has kept me up all night!"

"Thank you. That's really kind of you."

Rachel offered to buy the first drinks but Ffion winked and told her the honour was hers. They were settling in around a table when Rachel saw a policeman talking to the landlord at the bar.

"Bit early to escort me home, aren't they?" said Siân, "I haven't started yet!"

They laughed and, as Beth began to explain the mix up with Mrs Parry's blue rinse, they were still laughing when the policeman, with a policewoman behind him, approached the table.

"Mrs Fuller?" asked the policeman, looking around the table, "Mrs Rachel Fuller?"

Trepidation crept up Rachel's back and over her shoulders like the mist curling off the River Styx as she heard herself say, "Me, I'm Rachel Fuller."

"There's been an accident, Mrs Fuller. You need to come with us."

As the words 'blinded' and 'ejected from the Dome' registered in her mind, the Screen went black and Candy felt the bed rising to the ceiling.

As something was pressed over her eyes and slipped over her head, she began to struggle but the whispering voice calmed her.

"Don't move, please. You'll be safe. Lie still and scrunch your eyes tight shut. Please."

Even with her eyes shut, Candy could see the light and feel heat on her face. Sweat erupted all over her body but she lay still, hoping the voice was that of her saviour and not her executioner. She counted her beats, attempting to quieten her fear and give her mind space to think.

The light and heat ceased but Candy kept her eyes closed as the table lowered to the floor and continued slowly sinking. Without her sight, Candy's other senses heightened. The hairs on her arms stuck out from her skin as the temperature dropped and she heard a noise above her like a heavy object sliding into position. She tried to cringe away from what she sensed as danger. Slowly, she descended, bracing her hands and arms against the table, conscious that this journey might come to an abrupt end.

Alone in the dark she trembled, terror vibrating her nerve endings until a cry escaped her lips as the table shuddered to a halt. She lay still, straining her ears for any clue as to where she might be. From below the table, she heard a rhythmical tapping, three taps and then a pause repeated over and over. Hope replaced her terror with the knowledge she was not alone and she counted her beats.

Fear soon returned as the table began to tilt, not just at the top this time but the whole length of the table. The angle grew steeper, passing ninety degrees so within less than 100 beats, Candy hung below the table, the metal restraints that cut into her flesh the only barrier between her body and a drop she could not see. The pressure across her eyes remained. Where was the Whisperer now?

Cool air began to chill the sweat on her head as the table moved horizontally. Candy shivered as a rushing sound reached her ears. The rush became a roar until she heard a thundering below her and her body and face were spattered with cold, damp mist.

Candy's restraints withdrew and she fell screaming into the turbulence beneath her.

The Standing Stone – Silence Is Broken

Chapter 5

The Council were called and Adalbern, leader of the Tall Folk, agreed to join them. With her chores finished and the hairy stranger sleeping, Fern told Nia she was going for a walk.

"Don't be long," insisted Nia, "The tribe needs you at this meeting."

By the time Fern had followed the river and climbed the mound, a watery moon hung dripping in the murky night sky. It had passed from its full round majesty but its light set the Standing Stone sparkling.

Fern bowed to the Standing Stone, then leaned her back against it as she sat on the cold hard ground.

"Nia says the village needs me," said Fern, looking at the moon, "but what do I know? How can I protect us from men of war, bent on murder and destruction?"

She tipped her head back and a familiar tingle travelled down her body. Fern's world turned white.

As dusk turned to night, Rachel sat on the grass within the stone circle, her back leaning on the Standing Stone. The police had gone, finally satisfied she was well enough to be left, reassured by her promises of a friend to come and stay with her. Instead, she'd howled into the night within the circle, at the anger and injustice that boiled within her while a faint waft of burning pervaded the air.

The barn had been decorated with tinsel and chunky candles, now black and drenched by the fire crew's hoses. Within this setting of peace and light, lay Marcus' burned corpse. Rachel had clung to the arm of the policewoman. Accidental death had been quickly replaced by suicide when Rachel showed the police the letter left for her to find in the kitchen.

Pain and disbelief burned in her heart, mixed with anger at Marcus' betrayal. Rachel leaned back, tipping her head against the stone as tears scalded her cheeks. Moonlight brushed her face and she shut her eyes as the world turned white.

Though her eyes were open, Candy saw nothing before she hit the river. Fighting for breath, she splashed to the surface, feeling the surge of water pulling her along. Her shoulder hit something hard as the water drew over her head. Struggling to reach the surface, gasping and coughing, the rushing water shook her like a rag doll before dropping her screaming into a pool.

She bobbed to the surface and the water around her felt calmer, almost still and she clung to a dark grey boulder. Shivering, she began to breathe easier, silhouettes forming in her vision, lit by the silver grey light of an almost perfect disk in the sky. Tears mixed with pool water as Candy saw the moon with her own eyes for the first time.

Edging around the boulder, fearful of being drawn along again by the current, Candy found the rock was not an island but a promontory jutting from the

The Standing Stone – Silence Is Broken

shoreline. With bleeding fingers and aching muscles, Candy pulled herself from the water. She lay back on the earth, eyes transfixed by the sky. Above her, the moon whispered and stars twinkled and she smiled, despite the numbness of her limbs.

A need to get warm and find shelter rose in her and she crawled along the promontory, away from the water, to a single Standing Stone on a small raised hillock. Love, pain, fear, excitement and relief bubbled up inside her as she knelt before the stone and grasped it with both hands before Candy's world turned white.

Rachel opened her eyes to a cerulean blue sky, edged with pure white brilliance on every side. Sat on the grass she saw the two women she had met before, dazed and awestruck beside her. The Standing Stone shone like a beacon before them.

"Hello, again," said Rachel. "Hey you're bleeding," she added, crawling towards Candy.

Candy smiled as she reached her. "Who cares?" she said, laughing, "I'm out of the Dome, really out of the Dome...well, I was and now I'm here!"

Rachel took off her coat and wrapped it around Candy's shoulders where the remnants of a blue jumpsuit hung in tatters mixed with blood.

"You okay, Fern?" asked Rachel.

Fern nodded, grasping the hands of Rachel and Candy in a gesture of friendship.

"Welcome!"

The voice blasted their ears and they clung together, waiting for the thunderous echo to abate.

"Sisters, sisters forgive me," whispered the voice, "Look up, rise up, I will not harm you."

The Goddess stood before the women. Hair of darkest ebony hung to her shoulders while the crescent moon crowned her head. Swathed around her body, she wore a dress of night blue spattered with twinkling lights and around her waist hung the zodiac. A perfect rainbow enveloped her neck. Two winged lions stood at her sides.

"Welcome, human sisters, welcome to my world. I am Inanna, Lady of Heaven, Queen Moon and goddess of Venus, the morning and evening star. I am Ishtar, goddess of fertility, love and war. I am the Shining One, Mother of Deities and Lady of Battles and Victory."

Fern stepped forward, her hand outstretched to the goddess. "I welcome your presence, great and mighty Inanna. My village now sees me as a goddess and wish me to advise them. I am not a goddess and I am scared. How do I help them?"

Inanna spread her arms and behind her a yellow light began to grow. Her lions lay down, their heads upon their paws, as intricate links of chain mail and leather enveloped Inanna's body. From her waist, Ishtar took a single arrow with a bright emerald shaft.

"You are a goddess Fern, as are all women who follow the true ways. Take this arrow and you will know the best way to help your village. Use your gifts."

The Standing Stone – Silence Is Broken

"But I have none," insisted Fern, "I cannot see the future or stop the snow from falling, killing our animals, the old and new born."

"Your gifts are other," smiled Ishtar, "You will not be hasty for you know the wisdom of thinking before you act. You will not be complacent for you know the wisdom of being prepared. You will not be blinkered for you know that everything changes. Take your arrow, for it is yours, and be yourself."

Fern took the arrow, bowing to the goddess and sat down.

"You saved me," said Candy, approaching Ishtar, "Thank you."

"There was another."

"The Whisperer?"

Ishtar nodded. "He is the form to your force."

"Great Mother Binah talked about that," said Candy, "But I don't know who he is or how to contact him."

"He will find you," said Ishtar, "I see great changes in your world. You will need to fight and hold strong to what you truly believe, to what you want for your world in the future."

"I can make a difference?"

"You can and I have two gifts for you."

Ishtar brought two hands from her waist. One held a bunch of daffodils, the other feverfew. "Look to the earth and tend these plants well."

"Thank you," said Candy, taken her gift, seating herself on the grass, marvelling at the living flora in her lap.

"You do not approach me," said Ishtar.

Rachel shook her head. "I am comforted by being in your presence, Great Inanna, Lady of Heaven. When I look to the sky in the nights to come, I know you will be with me."

Inanna returned, her blue dress fluttering, her lions standing calmly by her side. She bent to ruffle their necks as she spoke. "You speak the truth but there is more. The blame is not yours."

"But I pressed him to talk, to talk about how he felt!" cried Rachel, sinking to her knees.

"He made his own choice."

"How can you know? How can you know I didn't push him?" Rachel covered her face with her hands and wept.

"I do," said Inanna, "and my gift to you will show you."

As she wiped her eyes, Rachel found a tiny lamp in her lap.

"The light from this lamp will show you the way," said Inanna, "Light it when you feel confused and are unsure of the path to take. Its light offers you opportunities that you may not otherwise see."

"Thank you."

"We didn't understand last time," said Candy, appearing at her side, "but we trusted the Great Mother and I've escaped the Dome."

"Is that good?" asked Fern.

"Yes, and someone helped me."

"After you spoke out?"

The Standing Stone – Silence Is Broken

Candy nodded. "Did it help you Fern, speaking out?"

Fern shrugged. "I've had to grow up, take on responsibilities."

"But you know you are supported," said Rachel, "by the Great Mother and the Goddess of the Moon."

"And us!" added Candy.

Clutching their gifts they stood together at the Standing Stone, breathing in the clear blue sky and the pure brilliance of the light around them. They each placed a hand upon the stone.

Chapter 6

The Council gathered and the villagers crammed into the round house to hear its words. A space was made for Adalbern, Geirr the translator, Adalwin and Adalbern's entourage.

Geirr repeated the words of the black hairy stranger. "Ten moons he has travelled. His village may only be five moons away."

"How is the stranger?" asked Adalbern.

"He is warmer," said Nia, "and he craves more food but my learning has taught me to go slowly, just with water and soup at first."

Adalbern nodded, conceding to her knowledge. "We must light the fires," he said, "and prepare ourselves to fight!"

"Wait," said Nia, "You presume we must fight. You don't know the fighting will come here."

Adalbern paused, thinking as Geirr translated. "We cannot sit idle."

"But to stoke the fires for casting will take much wood and many days to be hot enough to melt rock," said Nia.

Adalbern sat opposite Nia and he smiled at her words. "You know much of metal working."

Though her mouth twitched, Nia refused to smile. "I take an interest in all around me," she said, "especially those things that may disrupt our peaceful lives or damage the Land."

"There was no ill intended in my words, just acknowledgement of your understanding," said Adalbern, "but I say again, we cannot sit idle."

"Then teach us to shoot arrows from a bow like you do," said Fern.

She sat beside Nia as Adalwin did by his father.

"Is there time?" asked Adalbern.

"Would you really arm the village with weapons?" asked Nia.

Fern shook her head, remembering the words and wisdom of Ishtar. "I do not know how long we have, but neither do you. Maybe these warriors, this fighting folk will remain where they are through the winter. They have a roof and fire to warm them. They may not venture further."

Adalbern nodded while Nia shook her head.

Fern continued, the words of Ishtar resonating in her voice. "We must not be hasty or complacent but everything changes. Why not look to the skill of the archers, a skill Adalbern's people have?"

She looked to Adalwin as she continued. "First, there is a skill in the making of both bow and arrow. Would you teach these skills to us?"

Adalbern nodded. "These are skills we can teach."

"I say again," insisted Nia, "You would arm the village with weapons, Fern?"

The Council, villagers and Adalbern's folk all looked to her as she stood up.

Trembling but determined, Fern outlined her plan and her reasoning. "Our lives do not remain static. As the seasons change, so do we. Once it was just our village, Nia but now Adalbern and his followers have joined us. This news from the stranger is a sign that our world will change again and we must adapt to it. We must work together."

All around her, people were nodding.

"To be an archer takes time, I know, but this skill will serve us now and in the future. As well as making bows and arrows, the children can source the flat stones. We must decide and act upon a plan to defend the village while we learn to make and use bows and arrows. There must be ways to thwart any attempt to overrun us."

Adalbern and Adalwin started speaking together and Geirr attempted to translate. "Stakes and traps in the ground can be cut and dug and we can build guard huts to keep a lookout."

"We will not sit idle," continued Fern, nodding to Adalbern, "but we will not take war to another village. We will not stray from what we believe and care about."

Chapter 7

Rachel woke to the sound of a car's tyres on the driveway, pulling up outside. She struggled into her dressing gown and hurried to open the door as the first knock sounded. Rachel welcomed Siân and Beth into her home.

By the time Rachel had showered, dressed and fed Merlin the cat, wood was stacked in the fireplace, the burner was roaring and mugs of tea and a stack of buttered toast sat on the coffee table.

"I didn't...," began Rachel, "Thank you," she finished, tears welling in her eyes.

Beth shook her head and handed her a mug, "No need, no need, that's what friends are for."

"But you don't know..."

"And we don't need to," said Siân, touching Rachel's arm. "We saw the smoke last night. Everyone did."

"But we're here for you now," said Beth, "Talk if you want to or not, makes no odds. We're just letting you know, we're here if you need us."

Wiping away her tears, Rachel gave them Marcus' letter as she sipped her tea and nibbled on a piece of toast. They read in silence, only a gasp from Beth registering their understanding.

"So he's gone," said Siân, "The police found him?"

Rachel nodded. "Someone called the fire brigade and then the police were called. I saw...I was..."

"No need, no need," repeated Beth, "What about you? Do you have family to stay with?"

"Leave my home?" asked Rachel, "No, my family...I'm not in touch with my parents, I don't have...I'm an only child...I..."

A lonely, empty feeling rose from Rachel's stomach, scouring her with pain and fear and she let go. In the arms of Siân and Beth, two women she'd only known for a few weeks, she unburdened the shock and heartache she felt, secure in their selfless friendship and kindness.

As Siân made coffee, Rachel blew her nose and began to apologise.

"Stop that right now," said Beth, her index finger pointing, "What have you to be sorry for?"

"But it's Christmas Day and I'm such a mess..."

Siân tried to stifle a giggle as she brought in their drinks. "Well, if you weren't, we'd be worried."

"We'd feel we didn't know you at all."

"But I'm not usually..."

"We know! We work with you!"

A warm glow settled over Rachel. Tears fell but she smiled through them. "Thank you."

"What can we do?" asked Beth.

Rachel put down her mug and left the room, returning with a wooden box the size of a large shoe box, held tight shut with a leather strap.

"I noticed this last night, on Marcus' bedside cabinet but couldn't bring myself to open it."

"You've not seen it before?"

Rachel shook her head. "Not before last night."

They looked at the box and sipped their coffee.

"I want to know why," said Rachel.

"But the note..."

"Says why he took his life yesterday, not why we had the best of days before or why we couldn't have more. When I left...he was happy, excited almost and he'd asked me to stay, not go to work."

"And you think if you'd stayed, he wouldn't..."

Rachel shrugged. "I don't know, but it doesn't fit and this box was left out for me to see."

They stared at the box.

"Not wishing to state the obvious," said Beth, "but you'll not know unless you open it."

Whispering voices tickled her ears and gentle hands wrapped and lifted her body. She tried to open her eyes, to speak and move but she couldn't rouse and rested back into the sleep her body craved. When she awoke, musty smells filled her senses and her eyes watered from the smoke around her. A weight pinned her down and she struggled, her cracked voice crying out.

"Hush, child, you're safe," lulled a female voice, "You're safe now."

A light came closer, followed by the body of a thin woman with grey flecked black hair and striking blue eyes. A tooth was missing from her smile but it didn't detract from the gentle beauty of her face and Candy found herself smiling back.

"And you see!" cried the woman, "He saved another!"

"The Whisperer?"

"That's a good name," said the woman, "Let me help you sit up, you must be thirsty. I'm Anna." She hooked the lamp above them.

Candy shrank back. "You're a first born."

Anna nodded. "But there is no hierarchy here. We're not in the Dome now, this is a different world. Drink."

Candy accepted sips of the the sweetest water she'd ever tasted, tears escaping from her eyes at the bliss she felt. She sat back, propped up by more of the earthy smelling layers that covered her and she fingered them as she looked around her. Lamps hung from hooks on the walls all around the room, the light picking out the shapes of objects Candy did not recognise.

"What should we call you?"

"Candy."

Anna gasped, clucking her tongue before shaking her head and muttering, "Wicked."

"What?"

"Your name, child. It's a sweet confectionery, a special treat given to children Before when they were good. It's a beautiful name," she smiled and stood up.

"Don't leave me!"

"It's late, Candy and the fire needs tending to cook the meal. Are you hungry?"

Candy shrugged. "I'm empty," she admitted, "but Dome food...I guess I'm always hungry."

"Not any more. You are one of us now, one of the shining people and while you gain your strength, we will feed you."

"I wondered...can I...is it all right..."

"Ask," said Anna, "We will answer your questions the best we can. Oh, Candy!"

In Anna's arms, Candy let go. This was the moment she had waited for all her life. This was a safe place to ask the questions that crowded her mind and tortured her sleep. Here, outside the Dome, with the shining people, she would find the answers to her life.

As one village, the people worked together. Adalbern and Adalwin, with Geirr scurrying behind them, organised the men into groups and assigned them tasks. Fern's villagers and the Tall Folk travelled farther into the forest with Nia to supervise. She selected the trees to be felled and they bowed to her decision. Children of both villages, with an adult close by, scoured the land and filled their baskets with flat stones, suitable stones for splitting and every type of feather they could find. Adalhard, Adalbern's eldest son, began training the older boys to shoot a bow. Fern and three village girls around her age arrived for this training session and insisted, through hand gestures and facial expressions, that they were willing and perfectly able to learn this skill. Adalhard accepted with reluctance but Fern caught him smiling as the girls showed as much potential as the boys.

Three guard posts, tiny huts, camouflaged from view, created a permanent look-out for the village, occupied night and day by two people in each. Their job was not to fight but to warn the village if the warriors were spotted. Every able man, woman and child was shown and took part in the digging of the holes, traps filled with pointed stakes, covered by evergreen branches and dead leaves. Each needed to know the exact locations to prevent accidents and parents scolded less than attentive children, insistent on the importance of this knowledge.

As the moon shone full for the first time since the ritual on the mound, Nia and Adalbern called Council. They affirmed what had been achieved and set out plans for the following weeks but, as the villagers scurried to the warmth of their shared hearths that night, Fern felt the chill in the air against her exposed skin while the smell of the wind told her snow was coming.

They woke the next morning to a world turned crystal white. It was Fern's turn to take her place in one of the guard posts so she dressed quickly, foregoing a wash from the frozen bucket. Thick gritty porridge and a spoonful of honey warmed her belly before she set off for the outskirts of the village.

Fern had learned where the traps were by a triangulated position, using the village, hills and trees but she used a stout stick, prodding the ground before her as she neared each one, just to be sure.

The Land in its snowy mantle gave a different view through the window of the hide as Fern made herself comfortable on the skins on the floor. Clean, fresh and white, it was difficult for her to believe any murdering warrior would dare blemish its beauty. A noise behind her confirmed her guard post partner had arrived and a thrill ran through her as Adalwin sat beside her.

The Standing Stone – Silence Is Broken

In moments, she was in his warm arms, snuggling into his chest as he smoothed her hair and kissed her forehead. There had been no time for heartfelt embraces as they assisted the people to defend the village but, for this morning, they sat together, watching the view from the window for any sign of movement. They spoke a little, Adalwin having learned from Geirr a few words and phrases of Fern's language but mostly they sat in silence.

A movement on the hillside opposite stilled the breath from their mouths, until a deer's head stuck up, looked around and then careered off through the snow and they breathed again. Though a watery sun hung in the heavy, grey sky, it sent little warmth to earth and Fern and Adalwin moved often, changing places, standing up and sitting down to keep warm.

As the sun began its descent in the sky, Belle arrived with hot broth and the promise of only a few hours until nightfall and the end of their watch. She winked at Fern as she left, making Fern blush at the inference. Fern stuck out her chin and held her head high in an attempt to look stern and goddess like. As Belle's footsteps crunched away, Adalwin tickled her side, making her giggle and spoiling the effect. They devoured the broth, already congealing in its covered crocks and snuggled together, keeping the final part of their vigil.

As the light left the sky, two Tall Folk arrived with two lamps, one of which they gave to Adalwin as he and Fern left the guard hut. The men grinned until Adalwin spoke, short, sharp guttural words and they fell silent and bowed, backing away from him into the hut. Adalwin took his stick and holding the lamp before him, set off for the village with Fern clinging to his belt, the sack bag of crocks knocking at her side. Plumes of smoke hung in the air as they neared the settlement and Fern rallied her cold feet and legs at the promise of a warm fire and hot food. As the first house came into view, Adalwin stopped, put down the lamp and drew her to him.

"Miss you," he whispered into her hair, causing her legs to wobble, before he lifted her chin and kissed her.

That night, after settling the baby and crawling under her bed of skins with Rowan, Fern relived that kiss. She shut her eyes, breathing in, filling her body with the smell of him and feeling on her mouth his soft bristles and the warmth of his lips.

Chapter 8

Rolled inside the box was a sheaf of papers and, once unfolded, revealed medical records. Beth and Siân sat silently by her as words and phrases, 'depression', 'post-traumatic stress' and 'bi-polar disorder' registered in Rachel's brain. A knock at the door roused her from her reading but Beth was up and soon ushered into the lounge a policeman and policewoman, then she and Siân went into the kitchen.

Rachel recognised the policewoman and acknowledged her with a half smile before handing her the paperwork. "Go ahead," said Rachel as the policewoman hesitated.

When Beth and Siân returned with more drinks, the policeman was on the phone while Rachel conversed quietly with the policewoman.

Rachel briefly told them what the records confirmed. "The paperwork changes everything. Lifts any doubt of foul play."

"But the letter..."

"Could have been written under duress," explained the policewoman.

Beth raised her eyebrows. "You suspected..."

"No one, but it's our job to make sure."

"I can tear it down if I want," said Rachel, "The barn, I mean. They don't need to inspect it again." The charred picture of a skeleton was burned into her brain. She shook her head, trying to remove it.

"Nothing left?"

"The undertaker took all there was." Black, lifeless and unseeing, the skeleton leered at her. "You must go," Rachel added, "You've already given up your Christmas morning."

Siân shrugged. "I haven't had to peel veg, that's cool."

"And my lucky boyfriend gets a roast every Sunday so who cares!"

"We'll tell Ffion, if that's all right. She rang Beth this morning. She wanted to come but Beth had already spoken to me. No point her coming out."

"You've been so kind..."

"Don't start," said Beth, waggling her finger, "I've told you, it's what friends do. Now, I've a box in the car for you, just a few provisions in case the weather turns."

The tears came, followed by shuddering sobs. Rachel let herself be held and she listened to the gentle lilting voice that soothed her. Shaking and distraught, she let go. By the time she'd mopped up with the proffered tissues, Beth, Siân and the policeman had gone, leaving Rachel in the arms of the policewoman.

"I'm Natalie and I'm happy to stay as long as you need."

It was past midnight when Rachel left her bed to use the bathroom. Natalie had baked potatoes and cooked broccoli and carrots for their meal while Rachel had found a peaceful calm as she asked questions and was informed by the policewoman. Patient and efficient, Natalie explained the procedure for unexpected death and then offered practical solutions to Rachel's present dilemma.

"Dai the digger would help, I know, though he gossips like an old woman. You may want to create a version of events for him to spread."

"The truth's too terrible?"

"It's up to you."

Natalie opened the box to replace Marcus' medical records. "There's another envelope at the bottom."

In Marcus' handwriting, Rachel began to read his last Will and Testament before succumbing to quaking sobs and without resistance, allowed Natalie to take her upstairs and tuck her into bed.

Silence squashed the cottage like a 25Tog duvet. A scratching at the back door made Rachel jump. She turned on the kitchen light before opening the door a crack to an icy chill, a glimpse of snow and a miaow. Without invitation, a tiny white kitten with black ears, a black smudge on his nose and a black tail dashed through the gap and rubbed a cold, wet body around her bare ankle. Rachel shut the door and crouched down as the kitten skittered to the door with panic in its eyes before responding to the hand Rachel offered. Tickles behind his ears produced a roaring purr. Rachel went into the pantry and found a tin of tuna. There was no sign of Merlin but she put food in his bowl as well.

The kitten licked the bowl clean before wandering into the lounge and sitting on the rug to wash himself. Calm settled over Rachel after the trauma of the past twenty four hours. She stoked the wood burner and dragged her duvet and pillow downstairs onto the sofa.

By the back door she filled a seed tray with shredded newspaper before sliding under the duvet in the warm lounge and falling asleep. She stirred only once from her peaceful slumber as a heavy lump twirled itself into the crook of her knees and a small, furry body crawled into her makeshift bed and curled up on her chest.

"We are called the Taliesini, after the great bard and shaman, Taliesin. In the Before, he brought great wisdom to this Land, ways to live alongside and within the natural order of the universe."

"I've seen pictures of the earth," interrupted Candy, "and the Moon, the Sun and the Sea. Is that Universe?"

"Yes, but more," said Anna, "the stars are the Universe too."

"The sparkling lights?"

Anna nodded.

Candy dunked her wooden spoon in the pottery bowl and savoured her soup as Anna continued.

"I, and three others, are the Greeters. We live by the pool, close to the river and the waterfall. We greet those expelled from the Dome, tend their injuries, soothe their hurts and then conduct them to a suitable village."

"Suitable village?"

"A group of people who live together as a community. The Taliesini number over a hundred, since the birth of more children and the continuing expulsions from the Dome. Each person brings skills of their own and we spread these skills among the villages."

Candy shook her head before finishing her last mouthful. "I have no skills. I'm Candy Guard 14387. I stand and I guard a door. I have nothing of worth to share."

"You have questions or you wouldn't be here," said Anna, "You show an interest in the stars and the universe. These are valuable gifts to explore. You are young and healthy and female. You could be a mother now or in the future and your young mind is quick to learn. Maybe even more importantly, you had plants with you which we have not seen before."

"I left them at the standing stone!" cried Candy, making to escape the sheepskins that covered her.

"Hush, hush, they've been brought here," reassured Anna, "The bulbs have been planted in pots and the rooted plants, with sticks to support them. Can you tell me about the plants? Where did you find them?"

Sharing an experience was a new concept for Candy. She sat in silence, counting her beats to still her pounding heart as a vision of the Goddess Ishtar filled her mind. She began to explain how she'd touched the stone and been transported to another place and grew confident as Anna smiled and nodded at her story. When Candy spoke of Rachel and Fern, Anna's eyes grew round as if in disbelief but her smile encouraged Candy and she told Anna about Ishtar and what she had told her.

Anna clasped her hands together, pressing them to her lips as Candy finished her story. "You are a blessing sent to help us."

"A blessing? Is that like Comfort?"

"More, oh much more! There are those among us who can discern the full meaning of the Goddess' words but your plants must be important. We will look after them."

"And me?"

"You are now Taliesini, Candy. We look after each other. Now, sleep."

She took Candy's bowl as she spoke and removed the pile of sheepskins behind her, replacing them with a soft, stuffed bag. "Rest now and in the morning, you can meet the other Greeters. We will find you your village and take you home."

Candy lay in the dark. Though her body was sore and her muscles ached, her stomach was full and warmth filled her torso and limbs. Tears prickled her eyes as she snuggled deeper, remembering the pictures from the Screen of families round a table and she allowed herself to imagine what home might be.

Snow fell the next morning and continued all day and all night. Domestic tasks became difficult as the cold froze the water and clawed at the bodies of the villagers. Adalbern's village adopted the idea of Nia's and soon families lived together, sharing a hearth. Stockpiles of food and firewood were rationed and the animals brought in and fed with cut grass saved from the spring meadows.

The snow grew heavier. The very old and very young of Nia's village were kept near the hearth while those fit and able took turns to guard the village and work through the chores. As food grew scarcer, decisions were made about the future of the livestock and a pig and a cow were slaughtered for food and fat. Though the marrow from the bones was consumed by the old and goat's milk warmed for the babies, by the time the snow stopped, five Olds, the dark hairy stranger and two babies lay in the Council hut, awaiting burial.

Instead of snow, the wind blew, driving the icy cold into the huts, wherever there was a chink of light and Fern forgot what it felt like to be warm. Adalbern's village lost two babies, despite many families living in the big hut, conserving heat and warming each other so, when the wind dropped and the snow had melted to just a light muddy covering, a procession of people set off for the mound, carrying their dead with them. Fern watched the Tall Folk continuing to their barrow as the village dead were left in the doorway of the burial place, their souls commended to the ancestors.

Fern and Nia climbed the mound to the Standing Stone. Fern carefully carried a lamp she had lit from her home fire while Nia, resplendent in her fur cape, carried a skin of goat's milk.

"Great Goddess, mother of the Land, hear us as we honour you. Winter is upon the Land and we have lost kin to the ice and cold but we know, this is the way. Life begins our journey on the Land, while death begins our journey in the Other World. Life on the Land continues as, beneath the snow and ice, within your belly, Great Mother, new shoots are kept warm, ready for life in the spring."

Fern stepped forward with her lamp and knelt before the Standing Stone. "Great Mother Earth, this flame is for you to rekindle the sparks of life within you, to shine in the darkness and create good soil for us to plant, fish in the river for us to eat and new life to take hold in the bellies of our mothers."

She lifted the lamp high so the Stone sparkled as Nia knelt beside her.

"Goddess of the Land, we give back to you an offering of our love and devotion." Nia began to pour the precious milk on the ground. "Accept this gift so you may bless our female animals and the Land we tend for food. We have taken more from the trees to protect our village but upon my oath, once the ground is warmer, we will seek the saplings beneath the dead leaves and nurture them in your name."

Fern and Nia stood together as the final drops of milk seeped into the soil.

"Protect us, Great Mother of the Land," whispered Fern, "So we may serve you and honour your gifts, now and always."

As they neared the village, the smell of roasting meat set their stomachs turning. They hurried on, slipping and sliding on the icy ground, eager to sample the feast and get close to the fire. Adalwin appeared just as they reached the entrance of their hut.

He held out his hand to Fern. "Come with?"

Fern took the nod from Nia to be assent and let Adalwin lead her to his father's house. As she stepped around the seated villagers, Fern felt herself blushing

The Standing Stone – Silence Is Broken

despite the cold, as all turned to watch her. As she sat on the offered stool by the fire, she began to unbind her feet and legs, so numb were they beneath their covering but as she loosened the leather bindings, Adalwin knelt to assist her, his eyes leading her to his father.

"Adalbern seeks your advice," said Geirr.

Lord Adalbern nodded and spoke while Geirr translated. "Are the ice and snow to leave the land now? Is warmer weather near?"

Fern shrugged. "I cannot say for sure but there will be another moon's full journey before the weather warms, but maybe two."

After Geirr translated, Adalbern shook his head. "Two babies will be born before that time and animals too. How will they survive?"

"Our Olds and babies live and sleep nearest the fire," gestured Fern, "New born animals join them. We give new life the best start we can and venerate the old."

Adalbern nodded. "We should have shared homes earlier as your village did. Our fires are meagre as we ration the wood and our bellies are growling."

"Have you no barley or oats left?"

Adalbern shook his head, the mighty lord looking at his feet as he spoke. "There is little as most was used for brewing beer and animal feed."

Fern was aware of Adalwin holding both her feet as warmth and sensation returned within his hands.

"Father, arshamed," said Adalwin.

"Ashamed," corrected Fern, "but he mustn't be. We've lived on this Land for hundreds of moons and know how harsh the short days can be and how scorching hot and dry can be the long. I will speak to Nia about sharing our food. Your people must not go hungry. Without food, your people can neither look after themselves and animals nor protect the village. We will not let your people go hungry. What food were you given tonight?"

Geirr pointed to the pot over the fire where four pigs trotters bounced on the surface of the greasy water. Fern's face reddened. Perhaps her village didn't know how hungry the Tall Folk were but four trotters was not a sharing of a ritual feast. She took up the damp fur and began to rebind her legs and feet.

"They are not our responsibility!" cried Nia, "We paid them fairly with oats, barley and wheat for the goods they bartered. They should have been more careful!"

"How can you say that?" shouted Fern, "They guard with us, defend our village and share their knowledge. How are we not responsible for each other?"

"They are Tall Folk and we are not!"

"And we are all people and I will not sit by and watch them starve! I call Council!"

"You cannot!"

"Watch me!"

Weary but determined, Fern, with her sister close behind her, stepped over the dozing people in the long house and made their way to the fire. With dry sticks from her pack, Fern rekindled it until the fire was blazing. She dumped the block of ice from her bucket into the pot while Rowan opened the pack she carried.

The Standing Stone – Silence Is Broken

Smells of roast meat began to stir the sleepers so she quickly added it to the pot while Fern added sage leaves and barley.

Adalwin appeared, bleary eyed by the fire and peered into the pot. "You are our goddess."

Fern blushed, glaring at the giggling Rowan.

"No Adalwin," she said, shaking her head, "Not goddess, but I will not let my people starve."

"You said 'my' people," grinned Rowan.

Fern, though dizzy with hunger, having partaken of nothing until she had secured sustenance for the Tall Folk, still knew the answer.

"Our people," she said, taking Adalwin's hand, bringing it to her lips and kissing it.

Chapter 9

Days merged into weeks until Rachel found herself entertaining guests in her tiny cottage. Mr Brown, Marcus' consultant, Mr Feering, his solicitor and Mr Jansen, his accountant sat in the cosy, stone-walled lounge in their Saville Row suits, sipping tea and quietly conversing. Mr Feering, severe grey buzz cut on his head fortunately softened by youthful blue eyes, explained why they had asked to see her.

"Not only are we all familiar with your husband, Mrs Fuller but Mr Jansen and I worked for his parents..."

"And your husband's health issues began a long time before you met him, Mrs Fuller," said Mr Brown, "Sorry, do carry on."

Mr Feering smiled. "No problem, Alan, I just wanted to reassure Mrs Fuller that now her husband and his family are no longer with us, the three of us are privy to all the information and have all the expertise she may need in the future."

"Call me Rachel."

"Of course."

"But why did you want to see me?"

"Mrs...Rachel, not only did your husband leave his considerable inheritance of property to you but there are cash deposits that you should be aware of," said Mr Jansen.

"More money?"

Mr Jansen nodded. "It worries you?"

"Yes, I don't know..."

"May I say something?" asked Mr Brown.

"Go ahead," said Rachel.

"I've spoken at length with the police about the deceased but also about you."

"Me?"

"Because they were concerned. They told me you felt responsible, by going to work that day..."

"I hear you," said Rachel.

"As your late husband's consultant, I can assure you that you are in no way responsible. Wild irrational mood swings were part of his make up. No drugs or therapy were able to stop them."

He continued to elaborate on Marcus' mental health from his early teenage years while Rachel listened, her heart beating in her head, willing him to shut up and leave her alone.

"Thank you, really, I do understand but no amount of reassurance, at the moment, can comfort me. I was Marcus' wife but I never really knew him, do you see? Whether he killed himself or was still alive, I would be struggling."

"We understand how much of a shock this is..."

"Maybe," said Rachel, adding logs to the burner. "So aside from Marcus' mental state, would you financial gentleman explain in simple terms, what assets I've been left with?"

An hour later as she sat on the sofa, with Merlin on her lap, stroking the white kitten snuggled next to her, she hoped she hadn't been rude. It was kind of them to come, she knew that. Another trip to London would have exhausted her after the funeral and memorial service for Marcus and his family. They had been happy to leave the investments as they were, the difference being that now the interest and rent would be transferred to her account. She trusted them but, once again, she found the thought of such vast sums of money to be obscene.

She heard a car pull onto the driveway and made her way to the door before the knock sounded. She opened the door expecting to see Mr Evans with her grocery delivery but instead, a young blond man with a wispy goatee and shoulder length dreadlocks carried a plastic box towards her door.

"Mrs Fuller?" he asked.

"Rachel," she said, smiling despite her sombre mood.

"Rhys, I'm helping Mr Evans."

"How's Emma?"

"Doing well, I believe," said Rhys, putting down the box at the door, "Any day now, the midwife reckons."

"Give them both my best wishes," said Rachel, bending to pick up the box.

"I can bring it in, if you like," offered Rhys, bending towards her.

"You're all right. I'm bereaved, not ill!"

She returned a few minutes later from the kitchen to find another box on the step and Rhys standing, shuffling his feet by his van. He hurried forward to collect the empty crate.

"I'm sorry," said Rachel, "Had a tough morning which is no excuse for rudeness. How about you bring that box in and I put the kettle on?"

"Don't apologise, no need, no need," said Rhys, bringing in the box and following Rachel to the kitchen. "I'll not stop, if you don't mind. I've a delivery for Mrs Jones and there's freezer stuff in there. I'll take this box and bring you your parcel and letters."

"Parcel?"

"Yes, yes."

Rhys handed her a parcel and a handful of white envelopes.

"Mr Edwards at the post office came by and asked if you were having your usual weekly delivery today as he had a parcel for you. Thought it would save you a trip as the postage has been underpaid."

"Let me get my purse," said Rachel.

She sat staring at the parcel on her knees as the white kitten buried himself into her side and began to purr. There were also four letters with hand written envelopes and she recognised the writing on one of them as her mother's.

"Always questions," laughed Anna. She and Candy were on their daily walk. They had visited the pool where Candy had arrived in the outside world and were making their way back to Anna's home.

Candy laughed too. "I've had a lifetime to think of them!"

"And I don't know all the answers," said Anna, "but I do know you are well enough to make a home in your village now. Tomorrow, I will take you."

"What about books?" asked Candy.

"What about them?"

"Maybe I could find some answers in them, rather than having to ask all the time. The Screen talked about books that had answers."

"We have no paper books here," said Anna, "Be content with being safe, Candy. You'll soon be part of a community and you can learn from those around you."

Candy woke to the cockerel crowing and a delicious pink sunrise. By the time she was dressed, the wind had picked up and she accepted a patched coat over her mended boiler suit and jumper. Once their porridge was eaten, Candy bid farewell to the little house, her home these past weeks and followed Anna down the path to the river in borrowed boots. Though the sun was almost risen, the wind whipped at the water as they followed it down into the bottom of the valley.

"Who decided which village I should live in?"

"Not one person but many," said Anna, "I had some say as I've spoken to you most. You'll love Three Oaks. It's quiet, I suppose, but being on a hill, it affords a great view over the country."

"Are there other people out there, beyond Three Oaks?"

"I don't know but I doubt it."

The Standing Stone – Silence Is Broken

"What if someone was ejected from the Dome and found their own way out of the pool. They could be anywhere, living on their own."

Anna stopped. "Is that what you want, to live on your own?"

"No, I'm not saying that, I just wondered."

They walked on in silence, Candy stomping her feet in the muddy ground. She needed to ask questions. There was so much she wanted to know. She stomped harder. She shouldn't feel like this. She was out of the Dome, the goddess had given her a special gift and she was walking to her new home so why didn't she feel happy? Since her deliverance from the pool she'd felt a niggle of doubt and it ate away at her, a barrier to her happiness. However much she tried to dispel her worry there was something too perfect about the Talisieni and their villages.

As the river narrowed and began to drop steeply, Anna stepped away from the water and began walking up a well worn path through a leafless wood and Candy followed. On they climbed, the sun dipping as the path grew steeper and the trees thinning until a man in a ragged coat and felt beret stepped onto the path in front of them.

"It's you, Anna," he said, grabbing her arm, "and the young one is with you. They are waiting for you. I will come shortly."

As Candy passed the man she saw his milky white eyes and added another blessing to her list. Hurrying to catch up with Anna, three tall broad oak trees, magnificent in their leafless glory came into view before smoke tendrils in the sky heralded the village beneath them. Despite her previous doubts, Candy watched with interest as a typical day in the village unfolded around her. Children played in the mud with a small yappy dog while around communal fires, women prepared food. Rounding a corner, the regular metallic clang she heard turned out to be a blacksmith making horse shoes. Candy stopped to watch until Anna pulled her away. Some of the villagers looked their way as they passed, some nodded at Anna but the arrival of a new survivor of the Dome didn't sway them from their routine.

They entered a large house on a raised position at the back of the village square and were greeted by eight men. They were beckoned to wooden seats, covered in skins and blankets as the oldest of the men, who Candy thought of as Grey Beard, spoke.

"Welcome Anna and welcome Candy to Three Oaks, your new home. Charles and his wife, Ellen would like to welcome you into their home as their daughter."

Grey Beard indicated a thin man with a sallow complexion and a beaky nose who nodded at Candy in agreement.

"I don't know you,"said Candy.

"Of course you don't, child," said Grey Beard, "but soon you will. Charles and Ellen have two young children, Erin and Charlie and will appreciate your help in looking after them, as well as household chores. In return, you will have a home, food and company."

"So I'm not a daughter but a servant."

The Standing Stone – Silence Is Broken

"Candy! How can you be so ungrateful!"

All day as they walked through the valley to Three Oaks, Candy had struggled with her feelings and now finally confronted, the truth came out.

"Because nothing has changed!" she yelled, "In the Dome I was told what to do, without question or consultation and now, you are deciding my future! Is this freedom? I've brought life saving plants you tell me and yet no one thought to ask me what I want!"

"Selfish minx!" hissed Anna.

"No she's not," said a quiet voice.

A man stood up behind Anna and gently bowed. When he looked up, the skin crinkled at the corners around his milky white eyes in an otherwise young face. "I think you forget how much we suffered. If Candy has as many questions as you say, Anna, living within the Dome must have been unbearable for her. Candy, my name is Arthur and I live with my son, Ben on the outskirts of the village. He is about your age and came to me four years ago. Why don't you come and stay with us for a few weeks, get to know more people and then you can decide where you will best fit in here? Ben has sight and will be glad of your company and he can show you around, introduce you to people."

Anna, Grey Beard and three of the men began to argue but Candy raised her voice and spoke over them. "Thank you, Arthur, thank you for your kind invitation. I would be honoured to stay with you and be happy to help where I can to earn my keep."

Arthur and Ben's house was much bigger than Candy had imagined, a sprawling outpouring of rooms off a single main one. Doorways to other rooms were framed with wood and each had a different subject carved into the right hand side. She spotted an acorn in its cup and a tiny bird but didn't recognise the other carvings.

"So Artie always knows where he is," said a voice behind her.

Ben was short, auburn and stocky with hazel eyes and freckles on his nose. He grinned and held out a hand. "I'm Ben and I'm pleased to meet you."

Candy tentatively took his hand before he caught her off guard and drew her in and hugged her. "Welcome, Candy, welcome to freedom. No more Dome for us!"

Like a pair of feral cats, Candy and Ben circled and scoured the village. Ben knew everyone's name, what they contributed to the village and plenty of gossip in between. They scrambled up the path to the three oaks and climbed one of the trees, sitting aloft in its upper branches. Once the wood pile was stocked, the animals fed and watered and the seeds in the make shift greenhouse had been checked, Ben and Candy were free to go down to the river. Every day, they left the village and retraced the path to the narrowing falls. Sitting watching the water gushing by, Candy felt compelled to follow it, wishing to explore the new land it traversed.

"No one goes farther than Three Oaks," explained Ben, "There's nothing out there anyhow."

"How do you know?"

"Artie says the sickness killed them."

The Standing Stone – Silence Is Broken

"So the Dome was created to save us?"

"Yes. Artie says the sickness might not have spread this far yet but we have to be vigilant."

"What do you mean?"

"When the Talisieni meet, the scientists in Three Elms explain it all. The sickness comes on the wind so they monitor the wind direction."

"But it blows on the villages."

"It does but there is no sickness in it."

"How do you know and might there be one day?"

Ben shrugged. "The scientists monitor it."

"And you're satisfied with that?"

"It's their role."

Irritation gnawed at her stomach. How could Ben be so accepting after living in the Dome? Why didn't he question everything?

Around the table that evening as they tucked into the mess of potatoes, hard boiled egg and sweet parsnips in their bowls, Artie answered her questions about the scientists. "Most of them are alphas, given complex roles in the Dome. They were trained to spot abnormalities in cells. Our bodies are made up of cells," he continued as Candy looked confused, "The ones in our blood can tell a scientist a lot about our bodies and the environment we live in."

"Why were the scientists ejected?"

Artie shrugged. "Probably asked too many questions."

Snow retreated from the land leaving mud and a chill wind which whipped up the rain and lashed it at the houses. Firewood trapped under the snow was saturated so Adalwin led parties of villagers deep into the forest on their side of the village for days at a time, returning with skin wrapped wood which was often still too wet to burn. But they stacked the wood in the houses, allowing the warmth of the meagre fire and the human bodies to help dry it out so they managed to cook food and keep their bodies warm.

While the rain lashed down, arrows were fashioned, tied into bundles and stacked with bows in each house. Some were tipped with metal but the process devoured their firewood so the children set to knapping flints which could be bound to the shaft of an arrow just as well as a metal point. When the rain let up, Adalwin joined the trainee archers with his brother, offering help and advice as they practised in the woods. Fern loved her bow, made from a single hard wood branch, gently tapering toward the grip. She hit her target every time, even Adalhard raising his bushy eyebrows in admiration. As she and Adalwin walked back to the village that afternoon, one of the guards from the watch huts came running shouting towards them.

"There's movement on the hill top! Warriors are coming! Arm yourselves!"

"Hush, be quiet," hissed Fern, taking his arm. "Tell me quickly what you actually saw."

"Movement, movement on the hill top."

"Are you sure it was people, not animals?"

"Not sure, not sure, but they are gathering there, I saw them!"

The Standing Stone – Silence Is Broken

"You did well," said Fern, "Go run to Adalbern now and ask him and Geirr to meet us at the watch hut. I'll get Nia."

Once they had gathered in the hut, they peered out at the hillside where the other guard pointed but there was no movement or gathering shapes.

"We need to go up there," said Adalbern, through Geirr,"We can't wait for them to come down and slaughter us as we sleep."

"That's the role of the watch huts," said Fern.

"Until the guards fall asleep," grumbled Adalbern.

"Perhaps you should take a turn to watch if you don't trust them," said Nia.

Adalbern laughed as Geirr translated. "Maybe I should but tonight, we should plan how to get up to the top of that hillside without being seen."

"We don't know it is warriors," said Fern, as they walked back to the village, "It could have been animals."

"We cannot sit idle," insisted Adalbern.

"Then I will go with Adalwin," said Fern.

"No! You cannot!" said Nia.

"But I must," said Fern, "If Adalwin and I use this evening's moon to light our way, we can hide in the shadows and find out who or what is up there."

With Nia's words of doubt ringing in her ears, Fern set off with Adalwin as the moon appeared in the sky. If only Nia would trust her, treat her like an adult and not a child, decisions like these would be so much easier.

With her bow and quiver on her shoulder, Fern scampered after Adalwin as they moved from bush to shrub to tree, and made a wide circle from the village, to approach the hillside where the movement had been spotted. The air was cold, Fern's cheeks stinging as she tried to control her heartbeat but clouds of warm breath still rose into the night sky. They hunkered behind a rock. With hand signals, Adalwin suggested the route for their approach. Fern nodded and moved after him. As they neared the summit, behind where the warriors had been spotted, they took their bows and each notched an arrow. In silence, they waited, still as the rabbit.

Adalwin indicated for her to stay while he circled left. Crouched low, he scanned the grass and soil before beckoning her to join him. He pointed to a trampled path through the grass and footprints barely visible. They continued circling, Fern still holding her bow before her, tentatively following the path. Small trees clad the back of the hillside giving them cover but each snap of a twig made them stop and hold their breath. Down they walked as the path opened out onto a clearing. Signs of activity were more visible here and Fern tried to make sense of the footprints in the mud while Adalwin circled further.

"There were people there, no doubt of that," explained Adalwin, the following morning as Geirr translated for Nia and Fern, "but no more than three. Not a great band of warriors."

"But where are they now?"

The Standing Stone – Silence Is Broken

"The path from the clearing dropped down and then branched off in two directions. I could not tell which had been used," said Adalwin, "and I would not take one path and leave Fern to take another."

"There were no people close," said Fern, "I would have felt them."

"So, a scouting party then?" asked Adalbern.

"Maybe," said Adalwin.

"Adalwin and I will sleep today and return tonight."

"We must send more men, track them down," said Adalbern, "we cannot let them get away."

"But they are gone for now," insisted Fern, "The watch huts will warn us if they come back. Sending an army is asking for war."

"But what good are you two against an army?" said Adalbern.

"We watch, we do not fight," said Fern, "Please give us one more night."

That evening, Fern led Adalwin along the path to the mound as the moon appeared in her full and beautiful glory. Fern stood, arms raised, communing with the goddess of the full moon as Adalwin stood behind her, leaning on his bow. The air around them warmed and the hairs on their necks stood proud of their skin as the goddess bestowed her wisdom.

Fern explained as they circled the village. "She is the goddess of the full moon, of reincarnation, fertility and beauty. She will light our way and guide us while the sky remains clear and free of cloud. If danger is near, she will send us a sign."

Retracing their steps, they could see no different activity on the hillside or in the clearing. They chose the path that continued downhill and Fern followed Adalwin, her precious arrow notched in her bow. They crossed a stream, noting the footprints on both sides of the bank and followed the path up before Fern grabbed Adalwin's arm. The shaft of Fern's arrow glowed a brilliant green.

"Without coming into the light, we could not count them with accuracy," said Fern, as she and Adalwin relayed their findings the following morning, "but we guess there are ten or twelve men and women."

"Women?"

Fern blushed. "A shadow left the group and moved quite close to us. She relieved herself like a woman."

"But no one saw you?"

Fern shook her head. "They looked cold and hungry, clinging together in sleep to keep warm. An awning of skin was their only protection."

"We must gather our best archers," said Adalbern, "We can pick them off before they know we are there."

"No," said Fern, "We will not kill in fear of what we do not know."

"But there might be a bigger army on its way! We must at least remove this threat."

"No one has threatened me," said Fern.

Discussions and arguments continued until Fern could stifle her yawns no longer. "I understand your concern,

Adalbern, but our village will not kill without provocation. These people have not threatened us."

"So you will wait until you're murdered in your bed?" cried Adalbern.

"We have the watch huts to protect us," said Fern, wearily, "If you feel they are not enough, then increase the watch to three in each hut but now, I must sleep. Will you wait, Adalbern, will you wait?"

Adalbern frowned. His face looked lined and pale and Fern wondered how they were managing with food in his village. His beard and hair were shot through with grey hairs and Fern empathised with the lord trying to protect his people. Adalbern spoke to Geirr.

"My lord Adalbern will do as you bid. He appreciates your understanding of what you saw and doesn't wish to lose men if a surprise attack fails but he will not wait forever."

Chapter 10

A telephone call to Mr Feering's office confirmed Rachel's fear. Marcus' suicide following the death of his parents and brother had not only made local news but had made the daily papers. Marcus' parents had supported a number of large charities as well as local causes and been considered almost royalty in their area. Rachel confirmed to Mr Feering that her address was not to be given to anyone and he apologised that Rachel's mother had been informed.

"She was distraught on the phone," he explained, "I was in court and my secretary has only been with me a short while and did what she thought best."

"It just worries me it could have been a journalist. I can't cope with someone snooping around."

"I understand, I'm so sorry but Colette believed she was doing the right thing."

"It's not her fault but no more details to anyone. If someone contacts you, let me be the judge of who I speak to."

"Of course," said Mr Feering, "Is your mother a problem?"

"I haven't opened her letter yet or the other three letters...or the parcel."

"If you need any help, please let me know."

"Help to do what?"

"Anything. Restraining orders, investigation, anything. I'm here for you just as I was for Marcus and his parents."

The Standing Stone – Silence Is Broken

"Thank you," said Rachel, "I'll let you know."

Rachel's hand shook as she opened each envelope and read the letters. How these people had her address, she did not know, but all three were strangers, asking for money for a specific project they were passionate about. They were worthy causes, she admitted to herself, but her fear of the wealth she now owned prevented her from being generous. How could she choose? How much should she donate? Would they pester her if she gave a little and they wanted more? She shook her head as she opened her parcel. Within tissue wrapping she found a soft fleecy pair of wrist warmers and a set of delicate thermal underwear. She read the note and from the signature recognised the sender as the daughter of one of her mum's cronies but one who had been kinder and more down to earth than the others. Lucy Pinder's words were kind and caring, asking for nothing just passing on her condolences and offering a contact number if Rachel wanted to call.

Rachel sat stroking the white kitten as rain pounded against the windows, while Merlin sat on the back of the sofa behind them. Lucy's letter had moved her, a reminder of her childhood and the influence and manipulation of her parents but also a chink of hope that not all her friendships had been one sided. With a fresh mug of tea and the burner stoked, Rachel opened the letter from her mother.

She read it through then read it again before consigning it to the wood burner.

As the weather warmed, Candy and Ben helped plant out seeds now germinated into small plants and joined the hunt to restock the village's meagre wood pile. The weight of a heavy snow fall had brought down two trees close to the village so with hand made tools, the men cut branches into a manageable size for transportation. With her hands bound with rags, Candy helped drag the branches to the village while Ben joined the cutting party. She felt shy among these strangers, their faces bland and impassive and after two attempts to smile at the younger girls, she gave up when they glared back at her. She sat with Ben and the men to eat her lunch, a thick broth made in a communal pot, and as the days passed, they spoke a few words to her. Most of the men had sight, though a few had burned faces that had healed with raised ugly red scars. No one asked why she'd been ejected or spoke of life in the Dome but they explained how Three Oaks was the last village to be constructed, its proximity to the potentially tainted Badland, as they called it, making them the last bastion of civilisation.

"Have you been farther, past the rapids in the river?"

"There's no one out there," was their joint response.

"But why wouldn't you look?"

"The Badland is our barrier to the sickness," explained Ambrose, "Why would we risk infection?"

"But people might need help," insisted Candy.

"We cannot cure them and we may be infected ourselves."

Save for her red face, Candy showed no outward sign of her increasing anger. To voice such complacence and

The Standing Stone – Silence Is Broken

selfishness when another human being could be saved, seemed impossible to her. She viewed her time in the Dome as punishment, penance for the only crime she had committed, being born a third child within the Dome. With the Screen as her only source of information, she dreamed of tall trees, green grass and fresh rivers flowing briskly towards the sea. A life under a starry sky had been her focus. She loved the land now she lived on it but her idea of freedom was different from those around her. Ben liked to run with her, climb trees and scramble down to the river but he noticed nothing. Already the trees sprouted green buds, tiny white snowdrops blazed in clusters on the river banks and the variety of bird calls bombarded her ears while Ben talked, ignoring the new life exploding around him.

After checking on a mother and new born calf late one night, Candy used the brilliance of the full moon to guide her down to the river. Slipping and sliding down the muddy bank, she clambered back up and using a flint tool she had pocketed while helping with the firewood, Candy cut herself a straight hazel stick. Using it as a staff, she descended to the river again and began picking her way along the edges of the stony river bed. Twice she clambered back up the bank as the river turned and a jut of scrubby land barred her way but she returned as the river slowed and quietened and the moon dipped between the increasing band of trees. Rounding a corner, the river widened and on the side with most trees, it spread out into a large calm pool.

Candy backtracked and crossed the river and walked among the trees to the edge of the water. She sat while the moon reflected in the clear pool before her. Wrapping her arms over her patched coat, Candy talked to the moon and the goddess replied. She was right to respect and treat the land with awe and wonder for the changing seasons were the making of all life. People were a mere speck among the myriad of molecules, stars and planets which made up an infinite universe. They were not the makers, just one of the chosen, part of the life that this land could sustain. All was in balance here, force and form until humans believed they were worth more, wanted more and took more. The delicate balance was disrupted. Greed took precedence over the planet.

Candy asked the goddess about the sickness. A fireball erupted in her mind, so fiercely bright that she covered her eyes with her arm. Larger it grew, changing from intense flame to a vast cloud that formed a hole in the middle. Rising into the sky it sucked the debris from the earth and carried it with it. Ceasing its ascent, the cloud spread out like the mushrooms which grew in the forest.

Tears rolled down her cheeks as the earth, in the wake of the cloud, was pelted with the fallout and she wept at the images of burned bodies and desolated communities until her tears turned to anger. "Who did this?" she cried, "Who made this explosion and caused the sickness?"

The Standing Stone – Silence Is Broken

It took her longer to get back to Artie's house and there was movement in the village as she passed through.

"Where have you been?" asked Artie, sitting at the fire stirring the porridge for breakfast.

"Talking to the moon," said Candy, making her way to her sleeping pallet in the next room.

She woke a few hours later with rain pelting on the roof and Ben, his eyes upwards, placing bowls under the drips which were forming and trickling into the house. Removing her jumper, Candy went outside and stood in the rain in her jumpsuit. Once soaked to her skin and her hair sticking to her back, she came in and sat by the fire in her jumper as her jumpsuit hung steaming beside her.

"Been in the rain again?" smiled Artie, his hands carving at a lump of knotted wood in his lap.

Candy laughed. "I don't miss much about the Dome but even a warm shower sometime would be good!"

Artie winced at the mention of the Dome. He stopped his hands. "Are you happy here?"

"With you and Ben, of course. Why? Are you sending me to live with Charles and Ellen?"

Artie's gentle words comforted her. "Now, Candy, why would I do that? We like you living with us and I'm most grateful for all your help."

"Thank you," said Candy, "I've learned a lot about the animals and the land and I like being here with you and Ben but why won't the others talk to me?"

Artie chuckled. "New people, new faces, it disturbs them. From the conversations I've had, these people don't want any more surprises. Some were ejected like you and I but many were born here."

"You mean some of the villagers have never lived in the Dome?"

"That's right."

"It explains quite a bit, I mean, they have no idea how stifled, controlled and manipulated we were."

"Strong words."

"But true."

Twisting her wet hair into a rough plait, Candy wound it round her head and stuck in a wooden pin she had made to hold it. She watched the blind man pick up his work and using his fingers as his eyes, he began carving again. However hard she tried to quell her curiosity, questions nagged at her peace. What had Artie's role been within the Dome? He was an alpha, after all. Why had he been ejected?

"How long have you been here?"

Artie shrugged. "Could be five summers or ten," he said, "Never bothered to keep count. Are you dry?"

"Getting there," said Candy, "My jumpsuit isn't but I can put my coat on."

"There's a chest in the corner," said Artie, pointing, "Go look. There are clothes in there. Get dressed and take the butter to Jenny, the blacksmith's wife. She has pork to barter."

The freshness of the grass after the rain made Candy smile and she was still grinning happily when a man stepped into her path. She'd seen him collecting firewood but didn't know his name. Her smile vanished as she tried to walk around the man.

"Not so fast," he said, grabbing her arm and swinging her round to face him.

His face was big with prominent features and vivid blue eyes. He held her arm in a strong tight grip so Candy stood still. "Can I help you?" she asked.

"Now there's an offer," grinned the man, his free hand rubbing at his groin.

"Leave her be."

The voice came from behind Candy and she immediately felt the grip on her arm cease.

"I was just talking, passing the time of day," said the brute, dropping his head, his arms hanging to his knees.

"Well you've done that now, move on Norman."

Norman slouched away without a second glance. Candy turned to face her defender. The young woman was fair and slight but strength burned in her dark brown eyes.

"You must be Candy with the butter," she said, beckoning Candy to follow her, "I'm Jenny. I'm glad I found you."

"Thanks," said Candy, scurrying to keep up, "I've hardly been spoken to since I arrived here let alone saved!"

"He's just a simple man," said Jenny as they entered the back of the house next to the forge, "Simple mind, simple tastes, no thought of the consequences."

"Was he ejected?" A thought flashed in her mind that Paul might be alive and living in one of the other villages.

Jenny stood up from her rummaging through the cold store, wiped her hands on her front and put them on her hips. Close up, Jenny was little older than Candy but her face was lined and drawn."Have you learned nothing?"

"Sorry?"

"The past is behind us. We live in peace and contentment in this village. No one cares what happened before but you...you're always asking questions."

"I'm trying to make sense of the world, that's all. It's hard for me to believe that a new guard will be at my guard post and within the Dome, the days, weeks and months are playing out the same as they have always done."

"What does it matter? You're here now. Be grateful, make the most of it. We do."

Candy took the meat Jenny gave her and made a mental note to bring her staff with her when next venturing into the village.

As Candy encouraged a new calf to suckle that evening, she thought about Jenny's words and when her work was done, she set off with her staff down to the river. She'd peeled off some of the bark and rubbed at the spot where she gripped it, making it smoother and easier to hold. Below her grip, below her wrist she had attempted to carve out a circular moon only later remembering that the moon had other phases so clumsily she had carved a crescent moon on either side. After the morning rain, the night was clear and bright and Candy watched her breath as she made for the sound of the river. Fuller and wider than before, the water sang a joyful song as it crashed between the rocks. An owl called and Candy stopped, trying to hear a response above the noise of the river. Crossing to the still water was tricky but her staff supported her as she used her bare toes to grip the rocks. Down among the trees, stillness descended. Candy untied her boots from around her neck, rubbed her feet until they warmed and then put them on. She stood at the edge of the lake until the moon appeared, reflected in the shimmering water.

"Talk to me!" she called, "Tell me about these people!"

A shape darted through the air and landed on a low branch to her left. The owl watched her, turning its head one way and then the next.

"I can't talk to them!" she cried, "No one cares! Not about why we were in the Dome or about our future here. What is the matter with them all?"

The owl watched her, occasionally blinking and she sat down as images flashed through her mind. She was flying, like the owl but in daylight, over land which had once been forest but now was littered with burned smouldering wood. Then she flew over the remains of a settlement, a very large settlement where buildings crumbled and bridges lay in pieces over wide rivers. Her eyes stung and her throat burned and in the ruins of a church, she saw the lights. Tiny and flickering, a circle of flame surrounded a camp site. She flew on and saw more lights among the rubble, even though it was day, until the land ran out and they flew over the ocean. The depth of the turquoise water and the enormity of the mass below her made her feel light headed so she was relieved when she blinked and found herself by the calm water again.

Village life continued as the days grew warmer and the earth began to come alive. One bright morning, Nia announced that work would begin on the weaving house and she gathered helpers to her and set them to work. Children from both villages went out in groups of three with an adult to collect stones and Fern and her three charges, went down to the river. Finding the flat, grey stones was no problem but carrying them back to the village was hard work so Fern's working party made piles of the stones on top of the bank, ready to be collected and carried. By the time the sun was overhead, heaps of stones like mini cairns littered the bank as the children and Fern ate their bread and sheep cheese and dipped their cups in the fast moving river. As Fern took her place ankle deep in the water and began passing each retrieved stone to the waiting 'chain' of children, Adalwin appeared, calling a welcome from the riverbank.

The children giggled as Fern blushed, almost losing her balance in the water. Adalwin pointed to the piles of stones, uttered words they didn't understand before disappearing. He returned a little later with two men and they and Adalwin began to take the stones to the village.

Once her feet became numb, Fern climbed up the bank, sitting in the afternoon sunshine while the children climbed the trees around her and squealed and laughed as they played.

With the final piles of stones removed, Fern gathered the children and walked them back to the village. All were excited to see an outer and inner circle of stones appearing, providing the footings for the wall of the weaving house. That first day two long straight trees were hauled from the forest, the beginnings of the roof supports for the building. Once the door posts were in place, Fern and the children would help weave the lattice panels to be covered in mud, dung, and straw.

As the sun descended in the sky, Fern sat and watched the villagers, brought together by this new project. A feeling of excitement grasped them as they worked on the weaving house, already ignited by the first healthy lambs born a few days ago and a new baby safely delivered to her family. The past few weeks had been tense, more guards posted in the watch huts but there was no movement on the hillside since that first sighting. Even with this new task to be worked, the men hunted most days and the villagers were continually practising their archery skills. Adalbern was dissuaded from firing up the forge to make daggers and swords until the wood piles were replenished, repairs to houses carried out and the wood for the weaving house assigned but Fern worried this truce would not hold. She saw the swords carried by the Tall Men, sheathed but ready and she hoped whoever had spied on their village had left and would not return. As the sun disappeared the hunters returned successful and fresh meat was added to the pots of nettles, cabbage and barley and shared between the villagers, Adalbern and Adalwin partaking of this communal feast. Once food was eaten and beer drunk, the drums began, the songs and the dancing and Fern sat leaning against Adalwin, watching her people, contented after a long and hard day.

Once the children were bedded down, Adalwin took her hand and they walked back to the river with only a half moon to guide them. Through the trees, their path was unlit and in the warm soil of a vast rooted tree, the couple lay down in silence and darkness, exploring each other with tentative fingers and tongues. Fern was not the passive part of this love making, her yearning for Adalwin having grown to desperation and while he remained gentle and caring, she pulled him roughly to her as their bodies entwined. Her fingernails clawed his spine and she bit at his neck as she took him within her for the first time and he cried out her name as the ecstasy filled them both. They lay together, under Adalwin's cloak until bright stars shone through the budding branches and cold drove them back to the village.

Three days of dry, glorious weather were followed by a change in the direction of the wind bringing rain upon the village and driving those working on the weaving house under cover. The slatted panels were constructed indoors, cutting and splintering the fingers of those who wove them. Fern and Nia used herbs to sooth the wounds, grinding up horsetail collected from the swampy side of the river and mixing it with honey to apply as a poultice. As the wet weather continued, the wood piles diminished and those without sore hands recommenced arrow making while the children knapped flint.

On the morning of the seventh day, Fern awoke to shouts and screams and a dry bright morning. She clambered into her trousers, quickly binding her chest and arms and ran into the sunshine, grabbing Belle's arm as she ran past.

"What is it?" asked Fern.

Belle's face was red and tear stained as she pointed past the guard huts to the hillside. "They're back! The warriors are back to kill us all!"

Chapter 11

It was ten weeks since Marcus died. Ten weeks and four days. Rachel sat in a chair outside her back door as the sun warmed her face and the birds flitted and twittered all around her. Wearing pyjamas and a dressing gown, she hadn't bathed and her hair stuck out at all angles, uncombed and unwashed. She twiddled the thin gold ring on her finger as she sat watching spring arrive in her garden.

Having a plan had been her saviour in the past. Organising, making a plan and sticking to it, had seen her through her first twenty nine years of life but such a regime was now beyond her. A plan suggested purpose, a reason to move forward but however much she tried, her mind refused to see a future. Last night she was angry, at the world and at herself. In the past, she would take such anger and direct it into her next project, determined, focussed and applied to her task but last night's fury left her helpless, a tiny piece of flotsam, tossed and thrown by an infinite sea of despair. She tried to analyse her anger. Marcus had been a carrot of hope, dangled in front of her when she most needed to escape her family, grabbed and devoured as the answer to a happy life but he was gone, his lies and secrets with him. Was she angry with the universe for taking him or for bringing him into her life in the first place? There had been happy times, she knew that, but now even those moments of happiness were tainted by the truth of Marcus' illness and she no longer believed the words of love he had once spoken to her. Yet his death had left her wealthy beyond anything she could have dreamed with the opportunity to help others and make a new life for herself. Was she angry because of this? Was she angry her choices had been taken from her and a new set of decisions put before her instead?

She heard a car pull up the drive to the front of the house but remained immobile, unwilling to greet visitors. A knock on the door was followed by a second and then a few minutes later, her name was called and her back gate opened. Rhys, in ripped jeans and t-shirt, waved shyly to her as he stood by the gate.

"You found me," she said.

"I'm sorry," said Rhys, "I was worried, didn't mean to intrude."

"You're all right," said Rachel, "Fancy a cuppa?"

Rhys found a rickety deckchair in the even wobblier shed and they sat drinking mugs of milky coffee and nibbling marmalade toast.

"I'm not keeping you from your deliveries?"

"Not today," said Rhys, "Just you today. You're my last drop. Mrs Jones is in hospital. Broken hip."

"I'm sorry to hear that."

"No ones fault, no one to blame but herself I'm afraid. There's still been frost these past mornings and though Llyr goes up there every other day to bring in her wood, she fell on the path to the wood shed."

"Ffion said she was independent."

"There's independent and bloody minded, if you ask me, which you didn't but I've said it anyway!"

Rachel smiled, she couldn't help herself. Rhys' open, honest face and ways brought a calmness to her which she hadn't felt in a long time. "I'm sorry you found me like this," she said.

Rhys shrugged, his eyes crinkling in another genuine smile. "You weren't expecting company though it's a bit early in the day for a pyjama party."

Rachel laughed and with the relief of tension, tears broke through and the pain and heartbreak of grief and fear consumed her.

They lay beneath one of the gnarly apple trees as the sun shone at its zenith and she held onto Rhys hand. He'd wrapped his long arms around her as she cried out her heart, not trying to stop her but allowing the waves of sadness and anger to build, grow and flood from her tired, thin body. He spoke no words as he soothed her with strokes and kisses on her head and she felt safe and unafraid for the first time since Christmas. Once her sobbing ceased and she began to apologise, he'd stopped her with a finger to her lips and without asking her permission, led her indoors and run her a bath. While she sat on the edge, as the hot water filled the tiny room with steam, he teased out her hair with a comb before checking the bath, kissing her nose and leaving her to her ablutions.

Her hair smelled of rose, her skin of honeysuckle as she lay beneath the apple tree, refusing to let go of Rhys, fearing his departure would take with it her new found strength. He squeezed her hand and pointed with the other as a robin flew into the bows above them, tipping his head before flying off, returning moments later with a thin twig in his beak. To and fro he flew, sometimes with grass, sometimes a twig, nestling it into the space where two branches grew from the main trunk. They lay still, unwilling to disturb the diligent bird.

Rhys had brought in her shopping and put away her fridge and freezer food but fresh fruit and vegetables littered the kitchen table. That evening she made leek and potato soup while Rhys cored cooking apples which they filled with dried fruit and brown sugar before baking in the oven.

They shared their meal cross legged on the floor in front of the wood burner while Rhys spoke a little of the village, its people and why he had ended up there. "I couldn't afford to live nearer the University, so I cycle in from here but lectures have been shambolic lately so I'm better off working at home."

"You live on your own?"

"I wish," he answered, "No, I live in the old barn up at Hew Davies' farm. Not exactly salubrious but dry and I've a wood burner."

"It's been converted though," insisted Rachel.

Rhys laughed. "No, still smells of cow but Mrs Davies plates me dinners and I can use their bathroom when they've hot water."

"You don't mind?"

"Mind what? Me living in a cow shed? No, why, do you?"

"Of course not, I just wondered how you coped without home comforts."

"Luxuries, you mean and no, I don't miss what I've never had. I lived rough while I finished my final year at school, far preferable to home life, I assure you and then I spent a few years travelling before signing up at the University."

"Being homeless must have been hard, especially trying to study. Didn't the school help?"

"They did, as it happens. Found me a hostel for a while but those places aren't meant to be long term. They helped with a reference so I could work so I waited on tables at night and studied at school during the day. I remember one day when it snowed and the forecast was set cold, they let me sleep in the boiler room."

"Oh, Rhys."

"Now don't you go feeling sorry for me. It was warm by the boilers and they were taking a huge risk letting me stay. Those teachers gave me hope of a better future by ensuring I pursued an education."

"And Uni?"

Rhys chuckled as he licked the last of the custard from his spoon. "Still tough of course but in one more year, I should be in a position to spend the next few years finishing my PhD."

"That's wonderful, Rhys and after that, what do you want to do?"

"Not thought too far ahead, never do. Small steps, move forward slowly and new paths open up along the way."

After Rhys left, Rachel went to the wooden trunk at the end of her bed and pulled out her tiny lantern. Sat on the sofa with the little white kitten beside her, she lit the lantern and closed her eyes.

Candy and Ben continued to tend to the animals and nurture the newly planted crops but they didn't go down to the river any more. They joked around as they had done, Candy enjoying the teasing of her adopted brother but there was a distance between them which hadn't been there before. As the days grew warmer, new life abounded in the hedgerows, trees and fields. Candy watched everything, excited to be growing food and inquisitive about every aspect of the countryside around her while Ben hung around with the other young men of the village, not acknowledging her if he was with them. The young girls in the village huddled in groups, whispering and staring as she strode past with her staff, delivering butter and milk and collecting provisions.

On one of these trips she stopped on her way back, the sounds from the forge enticing her into its muggy warmth. She watched in the doorway as Bill's hammer shaped the metal, glowing red hot on the anvil before he plunged it into the water, clouds of steam drifting up to the roof.

"Get on those bellows, you lazy boy!" yelled Bill, through the steam.

Candy, frightened by his tone, scurried to the fireside and began working the foot pedal. Fire leapt through the coals, the heat scorching her face but she turned from its force and kept pumping.

"Enough!" cried Bill, retrieving the metal and setting it on the anvil again. As he raised his hammer, Candy stood back and he saw her in the shadows.

"You!" he yelled, "How dare you curse my forge!"

"You wanted the bellows worked," said Candy, shuffling towards the doorway, her staff between her and Bill.

"I didn't know it was you! Get out!"

"Why do you say such hurtful things?" she said, almost at the doorway.

Bill spat on the ground. "Because you don't belong here, that's why."

"I've only tried to help since I've been here," she insisted.

"Always asking questions and bringing up the past, you are," said Bill, "Get away and don't come back."

Tears scalded her cheeks as she ran to Artie's house, ignoring the jeering children behind her. She threw herself on her sleeping pallet, hiding her face from this cruel new world.

"You unwell, Candy?"

Artie's gentle voice broke through her defences and she sat up. "No, Artie, just sad."

"Why's that then?" he asked from the doorway.

"Bill the blacksmith said I was a curse and that I didn't belong here."

Artie nodded. "I see, well, those who work with iron are superstitious beings, not great thinkers. Of course you are part of the village. Three Oaks is your home.

The Standing Stone – Silence Is Broken

Come now, let's get some food on. We've visitors coming to the village tonight."

Once they had eaten and the animals settled for the night, they made there way down to the village, to the house Candy was first brought to when she arrived at Three Oaks. There were crowds of people, milling in and out but they made way for Artie and she followed him. Inside, a row of men and women sat along one wall on hide covered benches. She recognised Anna and smiled at her but Anna showed no recognition, continuing her conversation with Grey Beard beside her. She lost sight of Artie, then saw him take a seat along the wall and found herself coaxed to one end of the room with about twenty other young girls. Some she recognised while others were strangers but before she could ask any of them where they came from, she was pulled to the floor and sat in the dirt as Anna and Grey Beard stood up. At the other end of the room, she became aware of eyes on her as twenty young men stood waiting for Anna to speak.

"The cold days are behind us. Warm weather will be ours for the months ahead. Now is the time of the Partnering, ensuring our community continues. Those who have made pacts will stand and claim their man."

Six girls stood up, giggling nervously before walking down the room with all eyes upon them and giving their hand to a young man. Once the hand was taken, each couple stood before Anna and Grey Beard. As their clasped hands were tied with a thin cord the other villagers, packed in and around the doorway, cheered as they left the house together.

"Now those without pacts will be Partnered," said Anna, as the last of the couples departed.

Candy was ushered to her feet as Anna and Grey Beard took a girl each and brought them to the men.

A searing pain stabbed at Candy's heart as she was taken firmly by Anna and given to a large, smelly youth with sores around his mouth.

"No!" cried Candy, trying to free her hand, "No one told me about this!"

A hush fell over the assembled villagers as Grey Beard stepped up to Candy. "You have defied our wishes already and left Charles and Ellen without aid. Now, you will do as you are told!"

"Wait," said Artie, "Can't she choose, Anna? Can't the girl at least choose the man she's to be Partnered to?"

"Enough allowances have been made for this minx," hissed Anna, "She will obey our rules."

Grey Beard tied the cord around her hand and the smelly youth grinned at her with brown rotting teeth, as they were ushered through the doorway into the village square.

While Adalwin and Nia calmed the villagers, setting extra guards at the huts, Fern ran to the mound. It was a bright morning. Small animals scurried and birds called in alarm as she hurried past. She climbed quickly, arriving at the top as the sun peeped from behind a cloud and shone on the Standing Stone. Walking clock wise,

The Standing Stone – Silence Is Broken

Fern gathered her thoughts before standing in the middle. Closing her eyes, she whispered her questions, feeling the wealth of the wisdom of the past surrounding her. Within moments, she was climbing down the mound.

Grabbing her bow and quiver she called to Adalwin, pointing to the Council hut.

Once Council was assembled, Fern spoke.

"There are strangers on our hillside."

"Let's arm ourselves and fight!" cried a voice, quickly joined by roars of assent.

"We will not fight," cried Fern, "Until there is nothing left to do."

"What do you suggest?" said Adalbern.

"We need to talk to them," she said, "Will you help us, Geirr?"

Personally addressed, Geirr preened himself and looked to Adalbern. "If my lord Adalbern is in agreement."

"What's the good of trying to talk to them?" asked Adalhard, "They are savages, killers of women and children!"

Shouts followed.

"You know this?" said Nia.

"You saw the hairy stranger, you saw him!" cried another voice. "He said they killed his family!"

Nia, sitting beside Fern, wore her cloak of fur and when she looked at the owner of the voice, he cowered back. "We know another village was attacked. We do not know why or who attacked them."

"They wanted to take the village!" cried another voice.

"Then why kill the inhabitants?" asked Nia.

"To take it for themselves!" cried another, "They will kill us next!"

"Listen to Nia," said Fern, "All we know is a band of men attacked a village and killed the inhabitants but that is all."

Geirr translated for Adalbern. "That is enough. We cannot wait for that to happen here."

"Don't you think if they had meant to attack they would have done so in the night?" said Nia.

"Why stand on the hillside so we can see them?" said Fern.

Men talked across each other, arguing and shouting until Adalwin stood up. Geirr translated. "Fern, Nia, what do you suggest?"

Fern looked at Nia. "We need to find out the truth."

Fern walked beside Adalwin wearing Nia's fur cape. Nia's insistence that she wear it had embarrassed her but it hid the bow and quiver on her back. Adalwin carried his bow and behind them walked three of their best archers and Geirr. They walked towards the hillside as the sun rose high in the sky, until Adalwin bade the archers stay back. He, Geirr and Fern walked forward.

Their approach caused movement on the hillside and as they neared Fern saw five figures climbing down to meet them. Geirr mumbled, glancing up at the hillside shaking his head, sweat gleaming on his brow and his protruding ears glowing bright red. Fern's palms were wet as she stopped with Adalwin, waiting for the strangers to meet them.

A man and woman approached as their followers hurried to keep up. Their hair was dark, plaited into long braids which the man wore tied up on his head. Their skin was painted, including their faces and their clothes, save for the cloak of the woman, were tattered and stained. Both strangers had bright blue eyes.

Fern beckoned Geirr to her to translate. "I am Fern and this is Adalwin. We come from the village you see below you." She took her special arrow from her belt, holding it aloft by the shaft. "Why have you come here? If you're words are untrue, I will know."

Geirr's words were greeted by puzzled looks so he abandoned Adalwin's language and tried another until a third translation brought understanding to the faces of the strangers. They began to whisper between each other.

"Their language is close to yours, my lady. They are speaking of trust and honour."

"Tell them we want to talk," said Fern, "Ask them to sit and talk with us."

The woman spoke directly to Geirr who translated for Fern and then Adalwin. "They are afraid, my lady. They will talk here with you but they are tired and hungry."

Once he understood, Adalwin left Geirr with Fern and walked back to the archers. Two remained in place while one man hurried back to the village. Fern sat down and beckoned for the strangers to do the same. The man, his eyes tired and troubled, whispered to the woman but she brushed him aside with her hand and sat down opposite Fern. With Geirr's help, the stranger told her story.

"I am Mara. We were attacked. Warriors came in the night." She looked past Fern to the village.

"We did not attack you," said Fern, "It was not us. Don't be afraid."

"You say this, but I do not know it," said Mara.

Fern held up her arrow. "This is a magic arrow," she said, "Adalwin and I came to check you out the other night, back there on the hillside." She gestured as she continued. "When we were close, this arrow glowed green to warn me. Today, this arrow will glow if you or I do not speak the truth."

Mara's blue eyes looked startled and the man crouching behind her whispered and pointed at Fern. "Why did you spy on us? How can we trust you?"

"Our watch huts saw movement on the hillside," said Fern, "The villagers were scared. Adalwin and I offered to try to find out who you were." Adalwin crouched beside her and nodded to the strangers.

"Watch huts? We do not know of these," said Mara.

"In the cold season, when all was ice and snow, a hairy stranger came to our village. We nursed him as best we could for he was frozen through and he spoke of warriors attacking his village before he died," said Fern.

Mara and the man muttered together before she spoke. "Where did he come from?"

"He had followed the river for many moons," said Fern.

"We do not come from the river," said Mara, holding her head high, "We come from the sea."

When the archer returned, he brought two young men with him carrying skins of water, a jug of beer, food and beakers. The men behind Mara ran forward as he approached and, for a moment, Fern held her breath until the men pounced on the water skin and Mara barked out her words. They fell back, their eyes pleading.

"May they take one skin to the others?" asked Mara.

"Of course, take some food as well."

The man with Mara stepped forward, pointing at Fern and Adalwin, his face sullen and scared.

"Lugh trusts no one," said Mara, "Will you and Adalwin eat and drink first?"

"Of course," said Fern.

Food and drink was taken up the hillside while Fern and Mara talked. Geirr was fascinated by the painted woman, blushing a little when she looked at him. As the sun began its descent in the sky, Fern and Adalwin listened to Mara's story while Lugh continued to watch them with suspicion.

"You are very young to be the wise woman of a village," said Mara, dipping bread into her beer.

Fern laughed. "I am not the wise woman. Nia is my guardian and has been the leader of our village since my mother died. She is far wiser than I but I am learning."

Mara smiled. "This is good. We all must learn from our elders."

Fern nodded. "The Olds have a say in how our village is run. We meet as Council and they and Nia guide us. It is only since just before the snow that I have helped."

"Adalwin is different," said Mara, smiling at him, meeting his eyes with confidence and pouting her lips as if to bestow a kiss.

"Adalwin's father, Adalbern, brought his people to our village, looking for a place to settle. We live side by side, helping each other when need be," said Fern, taking Adalwin's hand as he smiled at her.

"He comes from the sea," said Lugh, pointing at Adalwin.

"From across the sea," corrected Adalwin.

"Our ancestors came from across the sea," said Mara.

As the air cooled and the sun dropped farther in the sky, Mara made her decision. "Would you allow us to be part of your community? Could we, like Adalwin, join you?"

"It is not my decision," said Fern, "but for now, I see no reason why you and your people should spend another night outside. Gather your people, Mara and Adalwin and Geirr will guide you. I will go ahead and speak to Nia and Adalbern."

"Guide us?"

"We too have been afraid, Mara. We have tried to defend our village, though all we want is to live in peace. There are pits dug and hidden to slow down an attack."

Mara caught Fern's arm as she turned to leave. "You may be young," she said, "but you are wise."

Chapter 12

Rhys visited Rachel often, sharing a meal, helping her to chop wood and allowing her to talk or cry. She rose each morning, lit her fire, washed and dressed and looked forward to him coming. Some days, she remained alone, working on her land, digging up worms for the robin or clearing rubbish and pulling weeds. The earth was soft and soon she had cleared a patch, ready for raised beds. She wrote a letter to Lucy, thanking her for her gifts and kind words but most days, she sat in the garden, watching the robin, alone with her thoughts.

The river didn't call out to her any more and she hadn't been up on the mound since Christmas Day. Her land, her barns, her orchard were disconnected from her. Only the cottage and the garden were part of her life.

Stepping through the door of the pub was like walking through a wall of fire but she made it, thankful that no one stopped their conversation when she entered. Beth saw her from the bar and walked towards her.

"Happy Birthday," said Rachel.

"Thanks, I'm so glad you came," said Beth, greeting her with a hug, "You okay?"

"Not too bad," said Rachel, "Just a bit wobbly coming through the door."

"You'll not need to do it for the first time again," reassured Beth, "Come on, we've good news!"

Dragged towards the noisy crowd at the bar, Rachel's instinct was to run but she hung onto Beth's arm and was greeted by smiles and offers of a drink. Siân hugged her and with a white wine spritzer in her hand, she joined a group of women at a table who welcomed her and broke the good news.

"Ffion had a boy last night," said Siân, "Almost eight pounds. Now that's a big bouncing baby!"

"Are they well?" asked Rachel.

"They're fine," said one of the other women, "She's tired, of course, poor love but she'll be home tomorrow."

"So soon?"

"If your delivery is straight forward," said another woman, "They kick you out as soon as they can! Had my Adam at seven in the morning and was home by seven that night!"

Talk continued about babies and births while Rachel listened in to bits of the conversations while looking around the pub. Beth was at the bar, her cheeks glowing pink, a tall man at her elbow who Rachel presumed was her boyfriend. He wore a well made black suit with a mandarin collar over a soft grey shirt and his fair mousey hair was clipped neatly. His cheekbones and jawline were chiselled like a male model.

Rachel nudged Siân. "Is that Beth's boyfriend?"

"The suit? No, her brother. He's moving here in a few weeks. Been working in London and is looking for a change."

"Which one's her boyfriend? Sorry, I just like to put names to faces, you know."

The Standing Stone – Silence Is Broken

"Sure, no worries. Where's he gone...there, at the back in the checked shirt."

Rachel tried not to show her surprise as she viewed the man pointed out to her.

"He's twenty two years older, if you're wondering," said Siân, "But she's happy with him and that's what counts."

"Of course it is," said Rachel.

"You never dated a much older or younger man?"

Rachel shook her head. "Marcus was my first real relationship."

"Well, don't knock it 'til you've tried it," said Siân, with a wink, "Drinks? Whose turn is it?"

The evening grew rowdier with renditions of 'Happy Birthday' for Beth and the whole pub taking their cue from this to burst into song at any opportunity. On her way back from the ladies, Rachel stood at the bar, waiting to order a lemonade, deciding she would go home once it was finished. She liked the friendly relaxed atmosphere in the pub, her smart jeans, boots and long cardigan making her almost over dressed but she'd grown used to her own company and the quiet of her cottage and felt a need to return to it soon.

"I'll get that," said a voice to her left. "I'm Oliver."

Beth's brother steered her to a quieter table from where they watched Beth, propping up the bar. "Two more, I reckon, then her legs will go."

"Sounds like you've seen her get drunk quite often?"

"She was worse when she was younger!"

"Siân said you're moving here."

"I am," said Oliver, hazel green eyes looking intently at her beneath manicured brows, "Decided it was time to get out of London."

"You live there?"

Oliver nodded. "Flat in Notting Hill," he said, "And I've worked there for ten years. What about you?"

"I lived in Kent all my life until I moved here last year," said Rachel, unwanted tears filled her eyes as she tried to breathe deeply and keep back her emotions. "What line of work?"

"Financial adviser," said Oliver, "Though I'm a trained accountant. Can turn my hand to either but the former is more satisfying."

"How so?" asked Rachel, sipping her lemonade.

"I can balance accounts, saving money for big clients but there's something more satisfying helping people manage their money, getting them set up for the future and discovering for them the best place to keep their savings. What about you? Do you work round here?"

Rachel shook her head. "I had my own hairdressing business in Kent with treatment rooms and my own staff and I worked for Ffion when I arrived here, helping her out before the baby but nothing since Christmas."

Rachel's hands trembled as she picked up her glass. She knew the question was coming and she was terrified at the thought of her answer.

"So what do you do now?"

Rachel took a deep breath and surprised herself at how easily she was able to answer. "My husband died on Christmas Eve and I haven't decided what to do yet."

The Standing Stone – Silence Is Broken

Once she said her goodbyes, Oliver insisted on walking her to her car. He began apologising again until she stopped him.

"Please stop, really, I'm okay. You weren't to know."

"But I just blundered in with my size elevens...can we start again?"

"What do you mean?"

"Hello, I'm Oliver. Can we go out for a drink sometime?"

"Oh, I see, no, no really, I don't think so."

"Okay, right, well I don't blame you."

"What?"

"I'm an idiot, such an idiot."

"Stop, please," said Rachel, tiredness weakening her knees, "It's not you, Oliver, it's me. This is the first time I've been out. I even have my groceries delivered. Please understand, I'm not up to meeting anyone."

"Then I wish you a good evening, Rachel and thank you for your company," said Oliver, reaching into his pocket, "and when you are ready to meet a friend for a coffee, please call me." He handed Rachel a shiny black and white business card.

Rhys came up to the house the next day to find Rachel still in her pyjamas.

"Bad night," said Rachel, by way of explanation.

"Take your time," said Rhys, his blond whiskery face breaking into a grin, "I'll get some wood cut and have coffee brewing in the garden by the time you're done."

Rachel lay in the bath, the slam of the axe a comfortable interruption to her thoughts. A smile crept across her tired face. She had enjoyed Oliver's company last night but she sensed he wanted more, while her Rhys, for that's how she thought of him she realised, was content with being friends, helping and supporting her as she battled through these first months of grief.

Coffee in the garden was accompanied by croissants she found in the freezer while Rhys told her about the paper he had submitted to the University and the news of Ffion's baby.

"I already know." She laughed at the surprise on his face. "I went into town last night for Beth's birthday."

"Oh, right," said Rhys, "I'm surprised but pleased for you."

"You don't sound it," said Rachel, pulling a grumpy face which made him laugh.

"I am pleased, glad you're feeling better," said Rhys, intent on pouring more coffee, "Hey, I brought you something, almost forgot."

From a carrier bag under his chair Rhys produced a tattered book.

"Saw it in the charity shop. Thought it would help to plan your land."

Rachel began looking through the book about setting up a small holding. She turned to the pages on vegetables, raised beds and poly tunnels.

"This is brilliant," she said, making Rhys smile, "I've been making a start, come and see!"

They took their coffee to the patch, marked out with string and covered in black plastic. "I began last year," she explained, "Planning and stuff and I've been over this section, digging out some of the weeds. I've a way to go, I know but this year, next year, at some point I will grow my own vegetables!"

"And I'm happy to help," said Rhys, "For a meal or two from the produce, of course."

"Sounds like a plan," said Rachel.

A wave of emotion rose from her feet and she stumbled, landing on the ground. Rhys bent to pick her up but knelt beside her instead, holding her weeping body tight against him.

"Oh Rhys," she wailed, "I'm so scared. I made plans before and look what happened."

No amount of struggling could loosen the tightly bound cord. Candy grasped her staff as she was pulled along by the stinking young man who chattered banalities as he walked. Much of his words were lost to her but she gleaned his intention of making a baby that evening.

Candy's experience of men was small but every one, except Artie and the Whisperer, had either tried to force their intentions upon her or decide her future by their words. Though Artie had tried to help, even he was compelled to obey this rule of the village and she hated him at this moment for not warning her about the Partnering.

Round the back of a house, they entered a cow shed. The smell of fresh straw greeted her and the young man lit a lantern and hung it on a hook above their heads. As th flame brightened, Candy saw a raised area at one side had been spread with skins and blankets and it was to this she was dragged. They sat side by side, Candy taking a slug from the jar she was offered as her mind worked overtime, thinking of a plan.

Dissuading his wandering hand, she asked if the cord could be loosened but the young man shook his head.

"Not 'til after," he insisted, with a wink.

Candy sighed and hung her head. "That's a shame," she whispered.

"Why?"

"I thought you would want to hold me properly," she said, "I thought you wanted to be my Partner."

"I do," insisted the young man, starting to unwind the cord.

"I knew you were kind," she said, smiling coyly at her Partner, resting her hand on his thigh. "We should have another drink."

With her hands unbound, she pretended to join him with each passing of the jug, giggling at his advances, feigning tipsiness until the young man staggered to the door to relieve himself. On his return he found Candy stripped to vest top and trousers, standing by the bed waiting for him. He made a grab for her.

"Wouldn't you like me to massage your back?" she asked, dodging out of his grasp.

"No more stalling," he slurred, "We must seal our Partnership."

"How do we do that?" she asked.

The young man dropped his trousers, the beer making his excitement less obvious. "Come here and I'll show you."

The Standing Stone – Silence Is Broken

He made a grab for her, one hand finding the waist band of her trousers.

"Oh not there!" she cried, "It's my bleed time."

"Oh no!" growled the young man, falling onto the bed.

Before he could move Candy sat on the bed, cradling his head to her and handing him the jug. Her other hand grabbed his manhood. "I'm so sorry to disappoint you," she said, forcing herself not to gag at the stench so close to her face, "I'll make it up to you. Have another drink. No one will know. We can be Partners in a few days time."

Candy slid from beneath the prone snoring young man, grabbed her clothes and her staff and shuffled to the door. The lantern was out and the cow shed in darkness as she opened it a crack. She tiptoed back into the shed, retrieving the stack of candles and striker and tied them up in her jumper. Around the village she moved in silence until her jumper also held food and a water skin hung from her back. With her coat tied around her, she set off for the river, stopping often to listen for pursuers but no one followed her and with a half moon to guide her, she soon reached the riverbank. Following the familiar path down to the pool, she stayed on her side of the river, almost losing her boots in the swampy ground.

The shocks and surprises of the evening continued to torment her, anger against Artie and Ben bubbling to the surface amongst horror and disgust at the Partner she had been given and the act she had performed to seal her freedom. Tears prickled her eyes as she saw Anna's face, full of disdain for her but she brushed them aside and walked on. Once she'd looked to Anna as a benevolent older sister, a mother even but her lack of sympathy for one of her own sex swept those feelings aside and Candy focussed on the great Mother, Mother of all and took strength from the guidance of Ishtar. The dark forbidden Badland held no fear for her as she had grown closer to the land and the plants and animals which lived upon it. The earth was her friend and she trusted that no harm would come to her.

As she walked through trees, a little way back from the river, she gathered dry sticks until she had a bundle which she tied to her back with string from her coat pocket. Hunger gnawed at her, nausea rising as the effects of the beer began to take hold of her stomach. Candy walked on.

Along the edge of the river bank, the trees began to thin and the river widen. She needed to sleep and her cover was disappearing so she retraced her steps to the edge of the thicker woodland and stepped into a silver world with a grey domed roof. The moon's weak light couldn't reach her here and she hoped she was hidden as she burrowed beneath a layer of dead moulding leaves at the base of an ancient oak tree. The heavy silence embraced her and she fell asleep. She sat in a grove of oak trees and the ground vibrated with a gentle hum beneath her. The trees around her moved and swayed yet she felt no breeze, just the warmth of the sunlight on her face as a mighty oak stepped forward. His gnarled face shone and though he didn't wear a crown, she knew he was the King of the Forest. She shut her eyes, breathing in the safety and benevolence he bestowed, trusting in his wisdom to guide her.

Her growling stomach woke her and she broke her fast and sipped at her water. Her head was a little muzzy but she felt more alert from her rest so while the cheese and bread fed her body, she allowed the sussuration of the waking woodland to feed her mind. Bird song trilled above her and mice and voles skittered around the forest floor as she gathered her possessions. Using her staff she poked at her hiding hole, spreading the leaves over her tracks. Taking a different path, she walked down to the river as the sun warmed away the chill night air.

She walked all morning, stopping once to eat and wash her face. As the sun neared its high point in the sky, a different sound joined the noises of the countryside and Candy hurried on while the river continued to widen. She saw the spray in the distance as the earth shook and thundered around her. She had seen a picture of a waterfall on the Screen. She stopped walking.

She ate bread and cheese as she considered her best option. There was no point going back. She would have to walk a long way to find a place to cross the river and maybe further to go round the falls on the other side. She could walk away from the river now but something held her back from this course of action. One option remained but could she climb down a waterfall?

As she walked closer, a tuft of trees to her right caught her eye and she stopped, wondering what had drawn her attention. Nothing moved, all was still so she walked towards them. They were set farther apart than the woodland she had slept in and ferns, mostly brown but some showing new green leaves, gathered in the hollows. Beyond them, dead and crushed grasses covered the ground, thinning out to leave tufted, grassy rocks. Moving carefully to the edge, the waterfall thundering to her left, Candy saw a narrow path between crooked gnarly trees and prickly shrubs winding steeply down and took the first step to follow it.

With her right hip leaning back into the rock and her staff in her left hand, Candy scrambled down the valley wall. Less than half way down she stopped on a ledge to drink and rest her aching legs before standing, stretching and resuming her descent. As she climbed lower, spring came up to meet her. Sweet smells of grass tickled her nose and gaudy crocuses trailed down the hillside as the land began to level out as it made its way back to the river. She walked on, the sun beginning to dip until she could no longer hear the falls and on a beach like inlet on the river, she lit a fire, constructed a makeshift spit and cooked the pork she had taken from the blacksmith's larder. Her mouth moistened at the thought of the juicy meat but she cooked it long and slowly until she could bear the smell no longer. She almost fell asleep in the sheltered cove but dragged herself to her feet, kicked over the remains of her fire and set off along the river bank until the light disappeared.

The Standing Stone – Silence Is Broken

Candy headed towards the trees, a forest of mixed woodland which spread out along the valley floor. Deep among the roots of an elm tree, she covered herself in dead leaves and fell asleep. She sat in an elm grove, tracing the ridged lines of bark with her finger on a tall elm tree. A brown bear appeared from behind the tree and she jumped to her feet but as she looked into his eyes, she knew this was just a dream. She sat down and the bear sat before her and she felt all he felt as her dream unfolded. She saw the Dome below her, as if she flew in the air, and it was tiny, surrounded by beautiful countryside of mountains, hills and valleys. She saw herself, asleep beneath the elm tree and her determination to look for others outside the Dome and villages, was ignited. Excitement thrilled her as she saw herself bringing lost people together. As her dream faded, Candy slept knowing that the life she chose for herself, was a change for the better.

Mara, Lugh and their companions arrived in the settlement as the sun dropped behind the trees and were welcomed around the communal fire to warm themselves and eat. Twelve adults and a toddler were all that remained of their village and two of the women were with child, one woman due any day. Nia and Agnes, from Adalbern's clan, helped the pregnant women into Nia's hut with Geirr's help, as the women were scared and didn't want to leave their own kind. They were reassured by Nia's gentle words and soon, they were warm, fed and comfortable, lying on Nia's sleeping pallet with Hugh, the toddler, running round them.

Adalbern and his followers joined the camp fire and Geirr was called upon again as Mara and the men recounted the story of how they were attacked. The suddenness of the assault and ferocity of the warriors sounded like the words of the hairy stranger. The men talked of weapons and fighting, blades and swords were drawn and compared and marks in the dirt were made, showing the new villagers the defences already in place. Though there were now twelve more mouths to feed, seven of the new villagers were men and Adalbern seemed pleased to have new warriors for his army. Mara and Fern sat and watched them, catching parts of the conversation as Geirr translated, sipping the broth from the pot and chewing on bread. Neither spoke but their eyes met often and Fern was glad of the understanding they had between them.

Fern took food to Nia as the new people were divided between the two villages. As she approached the tent she heard the familiar groans of child birth, chilling and exciting her at the same time. The gift of life was a precious but dangerous one but with the blessing of the goddess, a new life would be there to see a new dawn. Fern scooped Hugh into her arms, singing to him as she rocked and walked. His grubby little fingers grabbed her hair but his eyelids soon grew heavy and she tucked him into bed next to Rowan. The children in the village slept well that night having been caught up in the day's excitement like their parents but Fern could not sleep and Nia joined her outside by the remains of the fire.

"Thank you for lending me your cloak," said Fern, adding a few twigs to the glistening embers. "Mara believed I was the village leader."

"We don't have a leader, Fern. We are guides."

"Adalbern leads," said Fern.

Tired and grumpy she huddled closer to Nia.

Nia laughed. "Adalbern's people have travelled far from home so maybe they needed a leader to follow. Here we talk, suggest, discuss and reach our decisions together."

"You don't want the village armed."

"Neither do you but I compromised, as did Adalbern."

"But now the threat looks to be a real one."

Nia sighed, stretching her arms above her head. "No more than it was."

"How can you say that?" said Fern, sitting up. "The warriors have attacked at least two villages now."

"But they are moving away from us, along the coast."

"So we should drop our defences?"

"No, Adalbern would not allow it. You look unsure."

Fern yawned. "I want to believe the threat is gone but I don't. I remember a song about a river. Small streams and other rivers joined it before it widened to the sea. If these warriors took one branch of the river and found Mara and her people, they could take another and find us."

Nia nodded. She rocked, keeping warm. "I had not thought of that. How well is the village guarded if the warriors follow the river, do you think?"

"Not at all."

The following day, Nia called Council and Adalbern, Geirr, Mara and Lugh joined them. Agnes tended to the new mother, delivered of a tiny baby girl that morning.

"I do not think the warriors will come today, tomorrow or for weeks to come," said Nia, after recounting Fern's idea about the river branches, "But they, or others will come some day. I think we should plan for the future."

"What do you have in mind?" asked Adalbern.

"A ditched and banked enclosure," said Nia. Pushing the circle of people back with her arm, Nia drew in the dirt. She drew each house in the village as a full moon with a point on the top, a dotted outline for the weaving house and two more for the new villagers. Around the plot, she drew an outline and around that another, explaining with Geirr's help how the ditch would protect them and how they could defend the site with a tall, stout fence and gates.

"Where will all this wood come from?" asked Fern.

"We will have to travel deeper into the forest," said Adalbern.

"It takes days even now to come back with mature trees, father," said Adalwin.

"You could paddle down the river," said Mara.

The Council stopped and stared at her.

"Of course!" cried Adalbern, "We can make boats, cut down trees and then float them behind us as we paddle back upstream."

Fern saw the fear on the faces of the Olds and spoke up. "First we must talk to the goddess. Felling large numbers of trees leaves dead ground behind it. We must not strip the land bare but work with it as we do when we coppice for fencing and dividers."

Adalbern nodded to her. "You are right, Fern. This is about the future. We cannot take from the land without putting back or there will be nothing left for our children but with the village growing, we may need to clear land for crops anyway. How many with you can make boats, Mara?"

Mara laughed, her braided hair dancing around her head. "All of us, Adalbern. We are Boat People."

Fern sat outside her house rocking the new baby so her mother could sleep. Though the fingers which grabbed hers were tiny, the child was pinker now and her cheeks were starting to fill out. Rowan stood next to Fern, practising with her drop spindle, laughing when the thread snapped and sitting down to join the broken fibres. She chattered about the Boat People and how much she wanted to sail in a boat to the sea. Once her handful of sheep's wool was used up, she ran off to find Agnes and show her.

Fern watched as her villagers, the Tall Folk and the Boat People worked together. She saw Geirr hurrying between them and remembered something she wanted to ask him. Work on the weaving house was to continue but not the looms themselves, though all were told to look out for large stones which already had holes in them. This building would be home to the Boat People first, sheltering them this year as they worked on the village defences and boats. The door posts were in place and post holes were dug ready for the roof supports so the men were finishing the panels, while the women cooked food and prepared the wall mixture. A wooden cradle had been made, lined with pelts and into this straw, dung, mud from the river and earth from the land was mixed with their feet by the children. Fern giggled as one slipped over, disturbing the baby so she stood up, rocking her gently before placing her in a basket beside her sleeping mother.

Fern helped set in one of the posts before joining the women, collecting a leather bucket of the mud mixture between them and slapping it on the first erected panel. Mara came to help. As the sun rose and the day warmed, Mara took off her cloak, revealing her bare breasts which, like her face, arms and legs, were intricately adorned.

Men returned from hunting as the sun began to fall and everyone cheered at the rabbits they had caught which were added to the nettle and barley stew. The men joined the house building and before the light faded, three roof poles and two more panels had been added.

All the villagers gathered to eat together, sharing crockery with the Boat People as well as food. Adalwin, absent all day, came to sit beside Fern and she felt her insides quiver at the sight of him. Many nights had passed since they had lain together and Fern missed him, his touch and his support. Whenever he was near, she felt brave and certain about the world while sometimes, on her own, she wanted to hide from the pace of the changes around her.

Chapter 13

Rhys arrived with the planks in his van at 8am on Sunday morning. By midday, he and Rachel had two raised beds built and sat down to a well deserved lunch. Rhys' book from the charity shop had reignited a desire in Rachel to grow her own food so with that as her focus and an organic seed catalogue, work was progressing on her land. She had purchased a second hand mini digger too which could break up the earth with one clever tool and scoop it up with another. She felt happy in her boiler suit, Wellington boots and with a scarf around her head as she busied herself with her digger once Rhys had left. The robin followed her, dipping into the freshly turned soil to catch up a juicy worm. Even the little white kitten, Angel Face, joined her in the garden as she kicked off her boots and drank her tea. Merlin sat on the lid of the water butt soaking up the sunshine.

Thoughts of Rhys without his shirt on came into her head and she wondered if asking him back this evening had been a good idea. She'd offered to take him up to the mound and the standing stone after he'd told her about the spring equinox and his plan to perform a simple ritual and he'd been thrilled to work in such a special space. Sacred he'd called it. Though she lit her lantern every night, Rachel had not spoken to the goddess. Her meeting with Inanna seemed like a dream, yet when she stood outside in the dark beneath the stars, she felt a comforting presence surround her and she was content with that, but Rhys felt her taking part in a ritual to mark the day and night of equal length and to ask for a fruitful harvest was appropriate as she raised her growing beds and planted.

As she lay in the bath, a face rose unbidden in her mind. The face became a man and Oliver stood, naked to the waist, his torso tanned and chiselled and his hazel green eyes twinkling with desire. As she watched he became clothed in a tuxedo, holding out his arm as she descended a curving staircase in a flowing turquoise gown. Out of the bath she smiled at her reflection as she pulled on her jeans and jumper. She waited, impatiently, for Rhys, glad when she heard the familiar tyres on the drive. She opened the door to greet him and was shocked to see him attired in a belted green shift, grey trousers and a cloak held with a sculpted metal pin. He held a staff in one hand, with a large milky crystal set into the top and a wicker basket on his arm covered by a cloth. His dreadlocks were adorned with beads, shells and bells. She held a hand to her mouth, stifling a laugh.

"Are you ready?" asked Rhys, blushing under her stare. "Have you a lantern?"

Rachel ran indoors, glad to get away, giggling as she found her lantern and spare candles. "Why are you dressed like that?" she asked as they set off for the mound.

"These are special clothes for a special occasion," said Rhys, "Why so funny?"

"Not funny, just not what I expected, that's all."

Rhys stopped and looked at her, the lantern light adding sharp lines to his already angular face. He looked about to speak but shook his head and walked on. As they neared the mound and the path wove through the trees, Rhys began to sing, touching the trees with his staff. Rachel muffled her laughter with her hand. Climbing the mound, Rhys bowed to the standing stone before walking around the circle. He placed stones around the edge and set out his cloth before the stone.

"Can I just watch?" asked Rachel, kneeling beside Rhys at the cloth to lend him her light.

"No," said Rhys.

"Oh."

"You can take part or you can go home."

"Why are you being like this?"

"I'm not being anything, Rachel. You can laugh at me and what I'm wearing, but you can't be disrespectful here."

"You've a bloody cheek!" cried Rachel, standing up. "This is my land, I'll do what I like!"

"Shall I leave?" asked Rhys.

"Please yourself," said Rachel, "but I'm not staying here to be insulted any more!"

She turned to leave.

"Why can't you see what's before your eyes?" called Rhys, "The Land will help you, heal you and support you if you let it. It's part of you!"

Rachel hurried down the path, hot tears burning her eyes.

After an hour of sobbing, she heard his van start up and back slowly down her drive. She threw the cushion she'd been hugging onto the floor making Angel Face leap off the sofa and hide beneath it. His scared face, peeping from underneath did nothing to dissuade her as she screamed through the house, throwing crockery and books and clearing surfaces with a swipe of her arm. In less than five minutes, the cottage was trashed and with her energy gone, she sat on the floor among the debris and wept.

As a chill descended on the house, she realised there was no firewood so she slipped on the nearest coat and hurried outside to fetch it. Once indoors with the burner blazing she flung her coat on the sofa where it rolled over tumbling a black and white shiny card onto the floor.

"Hello? Is that Oliver? Hi, it's Rachel. How are you?"

When Candy woke the next morning, a light rain was falling. She gathered her possessions and followed the river downstream. The land was muddy so her staff was useful. She began to notice prints in the earth where the land dropped gently to the water. Rounding a bend, climbing between arching willow, she came upon a sheep who, surprised as she was, turned around and bolted away, taking with it another who had been grazing nearby. Her face glowed hot as she clambered up the grassy bank where she found more scared sheep and lambs. The rain continued to fall making it difficult to see but as she shielded her eyes, she could make out the roof of a hut or house in the distance. Uphill she walked, her staff pulling her along, as fatigue and hunger gnawed at her aching legs.

It was a house with a small barn attached and she called out as she unlatched the gate to the front garden. The front door opened to her knock. Decay and death flared her nostrils as she walked into a single room with a bed at one end and an open fire place at the other. Silence crammed into her head, poking at her brain as her eyes adjusted to the dark. An outline of a figure, prostrate on the bed, sent her stomach squirming. A quick scan of the other end of the room revealed jars, packets and tins on shelves before she dived back through the door and gave way to her nausea.

Round the back of the cottage, a single wooden cross stuck up from the grass and brambles and Candy hurried past it towards the barn. Forcing the door with her shoulder, she found bales of straw and hay piled at one end and tools ranged neatly along one wall. Sipping water, she sat with her back to the barn as grey clouds blocked out the sun. A fresh breeze nibbled at her ears, raindrops began to fall but all she could see was the corpse on the bed. Inquisitive sheep appeared over the hill but ran away as she rose to greet them. Gulping down the tightness in her throat, she selected a mattock and a spade from the barn.

As the half moon appeared hazy in the dark cloudy sky, Candy sat at the fire she had made in a rusting cauldron. From the shelves inside the cottage she had retrieved a number of tins. Once the rusty tin opener had been mastered, the third tin produced a creamy chicken soup. Heated in the embers, she ate it with a bent spoon. The warm satisfying meal dispelled her fear and sadness and as she looked up at the moon, hope began to return. Plans developed in her head as she tucked into tinned peaches, drinking the juice from the can as if it were life giving elixir.

She talked to the moon about the cottage and the people in it until the fire went out. In the barn, Candy settled into her straw bed, lulled to sleep by the baas of sheep, an owl calling and the tinkle of gentle rain on the rusty tin roof.

Days turned to weeks as Candy made her home. She swept first, from floor to ceiling, clouds of dust and dirt billowing around her. Carrying up water from the river, she washed the tiny windows and mopped the lime washed stone walls, allowing some sunlight to pervade. Caught up in this domestic bliss, Candy realised she was no longer counting her beats. As she busied around the house, clearing out cupboards, often thanking the previous occupants out loud, there was no need to check if she was still alive.

A trunk at the end of the bed held a multitude of cloth and woollen items and soon the cottage was decked in bright yellow and white checked curtains and she, in denim dungarees and a pink jumper which hung to her knees. The sheep grew braver, following her on her trips to the river. In a cupboard in the barn, she found salt licks, which endeared her to them even more.

Beyond the small back garden, Candy recovered the remains of a vegetable plot and green house from the choking weeds. She used her mattock to break open the soil and was soon joined by a vocal robin and a bossy blackbird. A large square tin in the kitchen revealed open, grubby looking seed packets which she diligently sewed and watered in her greenhouse, calling upon the goddess to give strength to her new plants. Further inspection behind the greenhouse revealed a pump, rusty and immobile but with a thick raspy file and some smelly oil, the pump worked, dispensing with the time consuming job of bringing water from the river.

Some days, as she worked in her greenhouse or sat talking to the sheep, she thought of the village and Ben and Artie but mainly she thought of the future and the prospect of making her home right here and one day, maybe, setting off to see if she had neighbours.

Late one sunny afternoon, Candy lay naked in the tin bath in front of the barn. Two lambs, Fluff and Cloud, now almost sheep, head butted each other in tumbling, noisy play and she watched them, laughing at their antics. A baa, followed by another came from the river. She turned towards the noise and saw more sheep and a man dressed in khaki with a rucksack on his back.

She rose from the bath, wrapping her towel around her and preparing to run.

"Wait, Candy!" he cried, "It's me!"

The Whisperer had found her.

Excitement grew as the villagers prepared for the evening. They decorated rings of twisted willow with flowers and leaves and Mara sat with a crowd around her, painting flowers on faces. As the sun began to drop in the sky, three tribes gathered to proceed to the mound, led by young men carrying flaming torches. They called ahead to the spirits of the Land that the people were bringing offerings and blessings to the Standing Stone.

A slow drum beat settled the crowd encircling the Standing Stone as Nia and Fern stepped towards it.

"Great Mother, Goddess of this fertile Land, we welcome you! You hold the balance in your hands, of dark and light, night and day and we say 'Bring in the light!'" cried Nia.

"Bring in the light!" echoed the villagers.

"The dark days are behind us and we look forward to the light! We honour and beseech you, great Mother, to look kindly on your people," said Fern, "Our village has grown. Dark times have led others in need of shelter to this place, and we all, as one, come to show our love and respect for you."

Fern broke a precious chicken egg and dripped its contents on the ground while Nia held up a stoppered clay jar.

"It is the time when the day and night are balanced in your hands, great Mother." She unstoppered the jar and drizzled mead onto the grass. "Bring us long days of sunshine to aid our work and make our crops grow."

"We call upon the faerie folk and the spirits of the Land," said Fern, "To bear witness to the commitment we make to plough the soil, plant new trees and tend to the abundance in the hedgerows. We hear the birds of the air and the animals of the Land and we echo their excitement as you bring the light."

Nia picked up her besom and held it aloft. "Before you all, I sweep away the darkness, the dark thoughts and the dark deeds, leaving room in our lives and hearts for the blessings of Spring."

Around the central fire, the villagers danced to the drums and shared their ritual feast before Mara stood and gestured for quiet.

"I thank you on behalf of my people for your welcome and acceptance of our tribe. Nia, Fern, Adalbern, please accept these gifts as tokens of our friendship and know, though we are Boat People, our commitment to peace on this precious Land is the same as yours."

Three rings of hammered gold were given, the villagers gasping and shrieking with wonder at the sparkling metal, the colour of warm honey, as it reflected and refracted light from the fire. Fern saw envious looks on faces.

"Thank you, Mara for these beautiful gifts. I shall treasure my ring as a symbol of friendship between our tribes as we endeavour to live in harmony with the Land and the other people upon it."

Acknowledgements

The inspiration for this book came from the wonderful countryside that surrounds me in my little Welsh farmhouse.

Thank you Peter Jones, writer, cover designer supreme, formatting hero and true friend.

Thank you Michael Mitchell for your amazing photos which always inspire me and your kindness in allowing me to use one for the cover. Find out more about Michael at: facebook.com/M.Mitchell.Photography

Thank you Mike, my life partner, for listening to my words and ideas as they flowed from my pen and for supporting me while I follow my path.

Thank you to all my friends who have supported my writing over the past two years, encouraging me to tell my story.

Printed in Great Britain
by Amazon